SINLESS
DEMONS

SINLESS DEMONS

A.K. KOONCE

TABLE OF CONTENTS

CHAPTER ONE
A Princess Once More
Aries

With another dab of adhesive, I stick one more glittering silver flower to the hard exterior of my right horn.

There. Perfect.

I tilt my head this way and that, and a small sense of petty accomplishment burns in my chest at the sight of the many tiny blooms that accent my dark spiraling horns. It's the first feeling that hasn't been rage or emptiness in days. I look like a godsdamn unicorn threw up all over me, but it just draws attention to the one thing my father has asked me again and again to hide.

He's ashamed of my hellish appearance. Well, I'm ashamed of every single thing he's done since I was a little girl, so we're eve—no. We're not even. Not even fucking close.

Because three men who I care—eh, who I'm decently fond of them not dying—are locked away in the demon's hold beneath the castle. They're literally lying beneath my fucking feet, and I'm not permitted entrance.

I seethe another heavy breath through my clenched teeth.

"The flowers complement your eyes, love," Krave says from behind me.

My gaze flashes to him in the mirror. He leans against the closed door of my quiet bedroom. The hard lines of his chest and the sketching tattoos that line his body are accompanied only by his glittering black wings and tight black jeans.

He watches me from a distance. Just as he has for three long days now.

Just like my father told him, I'm sure.

"Be sure to tell Daddy all about it," I say beneath my breath as I dab another little bloom and add it to the others. I'm one fucking glittering petal away from having my own horny garden, but I don't care. It's tacky as hell to look at, but I keep on adding them anyway.

It keeps me busy, really. Doing this petty bullshit keeps me from not thinking about how monumentally I fucked up.

I put them in danger. And they paid for it.

My jaw clenches. The only comfort I have is knowing that today will be the last damn day I sit locked in my room doing nothing.

I'm done waiting to see their fate.

"He asked me to ask you to glamour them again."

Krave shifts where he stands but doesn't dare take a step toward me. Not after what he did to me. He accused Ryke. He let Ryke take the fall for me. They all just let him be beaten at my feet and then torn away from me.

I don't even know if he's alive.

He was so bloody. Everything was bloody that night.

My attention slides to the golden crown resting on my vanity tabletop.

It's his. Everything in this fucking room is his.

It's Nathiale's crown. The same one I killed him with.

And they've shined it up like new and passed it down to me, the future ruler of the Kingdom of Roses.

I've studied the detailed crown enough to know there's a speck of blood they missed in the central opal gemstone. It's hardly noticeable, but I notice. I notice it all the time. My thumb brushes over his dried blood. I caress the cold metal and memories whisper through my mind.

My gaze slides over the white walls to the balcony doors, and I swear I can feel the cold breeze that flitted through this room that deadly night.

You did the right thing, Catherine says gently.

I hate how supportive she's been lately. She's been careful with me. Like she knows I can be set off now and not pause for an instant to let her take control. My body is mine.

Mostly.

And I won't be fucking changing the appearance of it for my father.

I lift the crown and maneuver it over my ugly flowery horns. The gold metal, the smooth gemstones, the sparkling flowers, it's . . . a fucking atrocious mess atop my

3

long silver hair.

"I'm ready," I say with a small lift of my chin.

"Yeah, you know he's never letting you out of this room with your horns, Ari," Krave says.

"Yeah, and I don't give a fuck." I stride from my velvet seat and meet him head on.

He doesn't cower before me. His lithe frame towers over me even with my horns, and my stomach dips from the way he gazes at me. The longing in his dark eyes is hard to look at. It's even harder to keep an impassive, fuck-you glare in place, but I wear it well.

"Move," I growl with as much hatred as I can find within myself.

It's misplaced. I know it is. My anger with him is this constant thing that my father puts between us. If my father didn't own Krave, I'd love him completely.

But instead, I despise him every time he looks at me. Because with every glance, he relays what he sees right to the one person I can never trust.

The long fingers of his right hand, the one with the tattooed crown, twitch like he might touch me. Energy presses between us and siphons into my chest. I swallow hard.

And keep glaring.

For a long moment, I watch him debate with himself. Smoke swirls from his palms like a nervous tick that he'll never admit to. I can't tell if he's about to give in to me. I think he is.

I think he might.

"I can't," he whispers.

Fuck!

4

Fucking Krave and his fucking ties to my father's binding magic.

My jaw grinds, and I have to calm myself little by little before I speak again in the lowest voice I possess.

"Krave, get out of my way, or so help me, I'll—"

"You'll what?" he whispers, his head tilting down so far that his words brush across my lips in a slow taunt of sensual dominance.

Something inside me reacts to something inside of him, and the moment that tingling feeling hits low in my core, I shove it away.

As well as him.

I grip his arm and twist it behind his back in one swift move, but like a dance, he twirls out of the forceful position, and we stand with our hands held, arms outstretched to one another, like long lost lovers preparing for the tango.

He smiles.

The fucking cock mongrel.

My nails sink into his tattooed skin, and I leap at him with all my might. Wind flicks through my hair. He catches me as we go down hard. His back hits the glossy wooden floor with a solid thud that knocks the breath from his lungs.

And still he smiles at me.

My legs are straddled on either side of his hips. His hands lift, almost skimming my thighs, but he holds them there around me as he clearly thinks through every move he makes. Before lowering his palms to the ground.

"Was there something you wanted, love?" he asks with so much insinuation dripping from his smooth-spoken words.

"Why—" My molars grind as I try to sort through the thoughts slamming through my mind. Why is he like this? Why did he ever make a deal with my father? Why can't life be simpler? "Why is your cock hard all of a sudden?"

"What do you mean all of a sudden?" His inky eyebrows lift with too much amusement.

He makes me absolutely crazy.

Crazy defeated. Crazy insane. Crazy confused.

Long fingers dipped in demonic magic carefully skim over my long dress as he seems to take his time touching me as well as thinking through what he wants to say.

He swallows so slowly, I can spot the way his Adam's apple works against his throat.

"Your father is in a meeting with his advisors on the third floor. First door on the right. It'll end in seven minutes. But if you hurry . . ." Thick lashes lift as he gazes at me intently.

My lips part as my chest warms like the soul inside me is trying to hold itself together, but it's a cracked and damaged little heart of mine. My palm lifts hesitantly. My fingers slip through his soft locks. A breath he was holding slips out in a wave of pent-up heat.

He's so beautiful. Hauntingly beautiful.

I can't help but lean into him. His hard chest and the metal that pierces through his nipple teases along my breasts as my light hair cascades around his dark. My tongue slides over my lips as his attention drops there. He watches every single move I make with a depthless hooded gaze. My lips brush his ear.

"Sometimes I want to kill you," I whisper. That smile

pulls wider as he nods to me. "And sometimes, I want to let myself love you so hard that nothing in these screwed up realms will ever hurt me, so long as I have your affection." My voice catches, and that arrogant smile of his fades from his face.

Shivers race over my flesh as his fingers drift up my arms. "You have all of my affection, Ari," he says on a pained tone.

My eyes burn with moisture, and I have to clench them closed hard before the emotions overtake me. He holds me to him, and I let him for just a second longer.

"Yes. I have all of your affection." I pull back from him, meeting his eyes. "And my father has you."

Sorrow and loathing creep over his sharp features as I stand and walk toward the door. He doesn't get up from where he lies on the floor. I don't look back at him.

I have a meeting to attend, after all, and I can't afford to make a late appearance.

Especially after all the work I put in with decorating my horns.

CHAPTER TWO
Family
Aries

The white gown I'm wearing is a tighter fashion than when I last walked through the halls of my father's castle. Things are changing here. The men walk around without shirts to accommodate their fae wings. And the women wear low-dipping gowns that don't caress their feathers at all.

It's all very sensual and stylish.

I blame the human realm for all of it. I don't know who specifically; maybe it's that Dashian family that's always on, maybe it's that Gaga woman, but someone in the human realm is to blame for this sexy attire.

And I can't complain.

The hem of the gown swooshes over the floor as I stride down the third-floor hall. And stop swiftly at the first door on the right.

He told you exactly where to go, and you didn't so much as mumble thank you. Catherine's voice haunts my mind, but I ignore her.

I have a dramatic entrance to make right now.

My back straightens. With my bedazzled horns held high, I fling open the door. It bangs into the wall, and I stand there like a discount bin goddess of nightmares, ready to receive mortal offerings.

The room is empty.

What the fuck . . .

I step inside, and the moment I do, tinkling laughter hits my ears. At the far end of the long room, past the many windows that beam with natural light, stands someone I haven't laid eyes on in a decade.

And seeing the little snatch again after all that time is far too soon.

"Aries!" Penelopia steps away from my father, rushing toward me with her layers upon layers of fine fabric clinging to her curves. She crushes her body to mine with a thud, and I just stand there with my hands held at my sides.

Again, let me reiterate, what the fuck.

She pulls back from me just to hold me at arm's length.

"It's been so long. I love your horns. They set off your wings." Her own teal wings ruffle behind her shoulders, and a flash of mental brutality flickers in my mind with the thought of rustling a potato sack over her still-chattering mouth and her perfect little wings. "Uncle Gravier was just telling me how you needed an ally at court, now that you're back. You need someone to make the people love you again. I've been his assistant for a while now. We should stick together." She ends that little prepared speech with a warm smile that doesn't meet her deep green eyes.

Krave does a far better job at hiding his true feelings.

She's a novice compared to my incubus.

"Everyone respects Pen. She's our go-to girl around the castle. She'll be good for you," a deep voice says, snapping me out of my murderous fantasies.

My attention flicks to my father, standing back in the corner of the room. His gray hair is smoothed down in long waves across his broad shoulders. He looks every bit a powerful fae king. As well as a severely disappointed father.

"Pen, why don't you leave us while you plan Aries' welcome back party this weekend," the king says in his commanding tone that leaves no room for argument.

A welcome back party. Right. He wants me accepted here. But not with these horns. So, I doubt the party will really be happening.

Penelopia rubs my arm once more before my cousin prances from the room like a sickness waiting to settle in my lungs.

She seems harmless, though. She's no longer the little annoying pest I remember as a young girl.

Maybe she is different now.

The king's gaze watches the door close slowly. Then he pins that attention on me.

"I asked you to glamour those things." He points vaguely to the lovely collage of glittery flowers donning the top of my head.

"What things, Daddy?" My arms fold, my head still held obnoxiously high.

Look me in the eyes, and tell me again how monstrous demons are. Tell me how those horned creatures will always be beneath us. The scum of the earth.

Tell me, daddy dearest.

"There are three demons held in the cellar of our castle. Do you care about those men, Aries?" He tilts his head at me in a challenging look I've seen so many times in my youth.

I have to be careful here.

For everyone's sake.

"I'll glamour the horns on one condition," I say suddenly, piquing his interest far more than the previous topic.

It works.

"Go on." His big arms fold over his crisp button-down shirt, making his black wings spread out behind him. He'll never change. Not his clothes. Not his mindset. None of it.

Be careful. Be careful. Be careful.

I cannot show interest in Ryke. I can't ask about his wounds. I can't ask about Damien's status or if Zaviar's been bound to anyone yet.

I must be careful.

"I want a demon of my own. Someone to do my errands for me. Krave's been a good guard as well as a kind friend over the past few years. Bestow Krave's bindings from you to me, and I'll glamour my horns." My chin tilts even more, and at this point, I'm almost looking at the high arching ceiling.

I make a point of holding his curious gaze.

He's skeptical.

But I know he wants my appearance to be accepted more than he cares about if I have feelings for the demon who loves me. It just comes down to who has the better poker face.

"Fine," he booms. "Take the demon. Hide the horns. And meet me downstairs for lunch in thirty minutes."

A wide smile beams across my face.

And for once, it's genuine.

CHAPTER THREE
Rules and Erections
Krave

I think—I think my heart just stopped.

"*You're* my handler?" I ask her again for the third time.

Perhaps I had a demonic stroke, and all of this is just a sinful dream meant to put me out of my misery.

That's not true. My sinful dreams are much, *much* better than this.

Ari still has her clothes on, for one.

Her confidence is like steel. Her spine is impossibly straight, and she lifts that delicate chin of hers even higher, as if that's some form of dominance.

It's not. But it's cute.

She pulls the silver pin from our palms, stinging my

flesh with the pain of the bonding magic instilled in that little needle-like weapon. I remember how much it hurt when her father did it to me. But right now, I'm beyond happy.

The happiest I've been in a long, long time.

"Yes. And as your handler, things are going to be a little different between you and me." She tilts her head at me, her arms folding hard against her smooth ivory dress.

Too many delicious thoughts spin through my mind, and before I can stop it, glittering smoke wafts from my fingertips. Images drawl themselves from my palms, relaying my thoughts in dark inky lines of swirling smoke. In my drawings, her mouth opens. Her eyes clench closed. No sound comes from the little erotic artwork, but we both know when the orgasm shakes through the smoke on trembling waves of wafting magic.

I clap my hands together hard and fast to dissolve the naughty image in a puff of black glitter.

But her disappointment is clear on her pretty little face.

"What did you have in mind, love?" I ask innocently.

Her steely silver gaze is still narrowed on me as I offer her a small smile.

"What is said between us stays between us," she commands.

I feel that binding command clamp through me like a weight written in iron and deposited in the deepest part of my soul.

Instead of the nasty feeling that normally turns my stomach when a command is given, a new feeling overtakes me: *desire*. It flits through my stomach with a twirl and a tingle, and I have to physically remind myself that she's not a fan of my cock spontaneously getting hard like it is.

It's a pity, really.

"Whatever secrets you hear around this kingdom are mine. I want to know every single detail that hits your ears. You're mine." A humming growl slips from my lips when she says that, but she keeps going. "You're *my* asset, not his. Do you understand?"

I keep the space between us in her little bedroom, but at this point, the erection straining my jeans is pushing so hard, it's about to burst right through like a surprise party no one wanted.

"I understand," I say lowly and stiffly.

Really *stiffly.*

Slowly, I clap my hands casually in front of myself, and her attention flits there in an instant. She blinks several times at the outline below my hips, and though she seems annoyed, her breathing increases. Her gaze averts but comes right back to my package.

And my heart's pounding so fucking hard, it's doing nothing but producing even more quality blood flow to the uprising south.

"Anything else?" I ask carefully.

"No more erections!" She shouts at random.

She was doing so damn good at being professional until that point.

Laughter shakes from my chest and skims over my lips as I watch her inky wings ruffle behind her. Her wings are her haven, but they also give her away.

She's not a blusher. She's not innocent enough to feel shame for her dirty thoughts. And she shouldn't. She just . . . gets her feathers ruffled every now and then.

I take two daunting steps toward her, and her body reacts by steeling her spine even more, if that's possible.

My fingers lift and instead of touching her long silver hair, I release a string of glinting smoke to caress her soft locks. She never takes her eyes off of mine, though. Even as I tell her in the quietest rumble of a voice, "You're my handler, love. But I'm an incubus. Some things inside of me are too powerful even for you." A filthy thought accompanies that statement, and I see it shine in her eyes the moment the same dirty thought flickers through her mind as well.

My index finger lifts higher, and I'm almost touching her cheek. The thin line of smoke caresses her skin, and the moment the contact is made, her lips part. Big gray eyes watch me with so much vulnerability, it fucking splits me wide open. My palm slides across her jaw, and suddenly, I'm leaning into her.

And she's leaning into me.

My mouth is drawn to her like her breath gives me life. My lashes lower.

Just as her lips part ever so slightly more.

And a cruel whisper slips out before the heat between us bursts into sparking flames.

"No touching," she says on a shaking tone. Her chest heaves against mine. For a single second longer, I feel every heartbeat she has to offer.

The command she gives is stronger than the demands of my heart. I step back. My hands fall to my sides, and there are so many thoughts clouding my mind, I have to shake my head hard to realize I'm still hovering over her. I linger long enough to see the fear in her eyes. I don't know if it's fear that I won't listen . . . or that she'll break her own rule herself.

I force my spine to straighten, and it's even harder for me to force the smile to my lips.

The lust that was just dancing in my stomach is leaden and sickly now.

I keep smiling.

"What now, my Princess?" The title is foreign on my tongue, and I want nothing more than to call her all the sweet things my heart always feels, but I have to tramp that back down. I have to find a distance between us.

Gods knows she has.

"Now, we go to lunch." Her wings ruffle behind her small shoulders, and the way she looks away from me and walks out expecting me to follow is like a knife sliding into my heart over and over and over again.

Pain is all I feel.

And yet, I smile.

CHAPTER FOUR
Wasted Time
Aries

In the quiet hall, I pause just outside my door. Krave's footfalls halt the moment mine do. My breath catches as confusing emotions tumble around inside of me.

Someday, things won't be such a mess between us. My life won't be such a mess.

Someday.

I exhale slowly, and just as I'm about to take another step, a voice calls out to me from the shadows in the far corner.

"Don't forget to lose the horns, Aries. Wouldn't want to upset daddy dearest." The mysterious voice is a scuttling sound, like cold wind slipping through cracks in a wall.

I'd recognize Sev's tone with or without the

darkness, though.

Krave steps toward the voice and the nothingness. A Shadow Guard isn't likely to out himself, but I guess we always look after our own.

My hand lifts, and I stop Krave's deadly stride before he can rip apart the shadows looking for an unseen threat.

I nod to Sev.

He's right.

There's a small tremble in my fingers as I lightly slide my fingertips up the long curve of the onyx horns. It's odd but . . . I like them. They feel like I've had them all my life, and I've just now grown into them.

Just to be told to hide them away.

"Ari," Krave whispers gently.

I peer at him out of the corner of my eye, and he's entirely focused on the top of my head. Sadness shines in his inky gaze. My heart pulls. I'm more connected with him and with Damien and Ryke because of my new appearance. It isn't just horns, though. I'll glamour them, sure. But it won't change how I feel.

It won't change what I am.

That's true, Catherine says, all too sweetly.

I don't know why I can handle her better when she's a cunt. I can't even call her that now. Gods, I'll have to start calling her Catherine the Kind.

Or just Catherine, she whispers.

My eyes close, and with a swift twirl of my glamour, the horns are gone. They're there but they're not. I feel them. I sense the weight of them, but it's more like a phantom feeling.

They're gone.

The sound of Krave clearing his throat just confirms what I already know.

"Sev, I'll see you tonight."

"I'm sorry, what?" Krave says as soon as the words leave my mouth.

"Oh, I look forward to it, Ari," the unseen man says from the depths of the shadows.

I ignore them both and continue on. My gown sways over the glossy floorboards, and every step I take is like I'm walking back in time.

I'm the youngest Princess of the Kingdom of Roses once more.

And I still fucking hate it.

***

"You're late," my father says as Krave oddly pulls out my chair for me.

There's a brief moment of awkwardness where I'm looking at the incubus, and he's aloofly looking anywhere but at me. With a small smile to him, I gracefully slip into the cushioned red seat. He jars me forward hard until my ribs hit the table, and the wind is knocked out of me.

I have to strain to look over the high back of the chair and give him a good glare.

He doesn't meet my eyes.

Because I'm his handler.

Not his friend. Not his mate. Not even his enemy.

I swallow that thought down and face the small dining table. Father sits at the far end across from me. My cousin is to my left, and my mother is to my right. One of them beams a cheery smile at me, the other . . . the other hasn't looked at me since I killed her son.

A heaviness settles in my stomach, and I don't care to eat the food decorating the table, but I take small sips of water for the first few lingering minutes.

"Uncle Gravier suggested I get a good demon for protection, just like you." Pen tilts her head at me until my attention slowly shifts to her.

I blink but say nothing.

Saying nothing is the safe alternative here.

"Every girl needs protection," my father says in his booming tone that echoes through the large dimly-lit room. "We have plenty of fine demons who need handlers, too. They'd be honored to have a sweet owner like yourself."

My jaw clenches.

I blink and say nothing.

Without thought, I trade my water out for wine, and I'm no longer sipping it, but downing it as fast as the demon waiter can pour it.

"Aries, I think that's quite enough." Father commands.

But he doesn't own me. He can't bind me. Not like his other pets.

I motion to the inside of the empty silver goblet, and the quiet waiter hesitates but pours me another. When it's gone, I motion again. Pour. Drink. Motion. Pour. Dribble down my chin. Clink the side with my nail. Pour. Cough some up when it goes down the wrong hole. Vaguely clatter my nails against the shining metal. Pour. Slosh red wine over the rim of the cup—

"Enough!" The word rains down over the room.

The waiter steps back like he, too, is a member of the Shadow Guard.

"Krave, take Aries back to her room. Get her some water and don't let her out until she's found her senses again." The orders come out one after the other, but I smile to myself when I realize his error.

Someone else is just a bit faster than me.

"I'm terribly sorry, my King, but . . . you're not my handler," Krave says on the smooth taunting tone of his.

My heart skips a beat for some odd reason that I don't understand.

I shove back from the table. My gaze holds the familiar gray eyes across from me, and I smile softly before walking away from them all.

I accomplished nothing, but it feels like so much all at the same time. It's so much that my heartbeat pounds with every quick step I take back to my room. I pass the crimson roses in their vases at every corner, I pass the line of formal armory, I even pass Sev, and I never once pause to see any of it.

My pulse speeds with warmth spreading through my chest. On quick steps, I enter the privacy of my bedroom, and I don't even wait for Krave to close the door behind himself before my fingers are slipping through his soft inky locks.

And then my lips slam to his.

His brows lift as I close my eyes, and a beat of time passes with his hands held platonically in the air before he clamps his palms around my hips and spins us so I'm pinned against the door by his hips alone.

The moment my lips part, his tongue meets mine, ready and hungry. Every part of me reacts, my body shifts, but really, it's just my hips shifting against his. A groan hums from his throat, and he pulls back with a shaking breath leaving his lungs.

"This feels suspiciously like touching, love," he whispers with a smile.

A real smile.

A smile that sears my soul with branding heat.

My head tilts back, and I search his dark eyes. I want him so damn bad. I want—I want something neither of us have.

And that's trust.

"There's a temporary rule." My words fan against his mouth.

"Oh?" His dark hair falls into his eyes as he cocks his head at me. "What's that?"

"For the next thirty seconds, no rules exist between us," I tell him with my heart soaring and breaking all at the same time.

I want to forget for a moment how completely ruined our lives are.

I want him to make me forget everything but how he makes me feel when I'm near him.

I want—I want him.

His palms slide beneath my thighs as his nails dig in nice and deep before lifting me and wrapping my legs around his hips. A tearing gasp of a sigh shakes from my lips, and he just eats it right up as he leans in close. "You forget just what I can do in such a short time, Ari," he says on a deliciously gravelly tone, his hips rocking subtly into mine.

My heart hammers against my chest. I stare down on him, wide-eyed and waiting.

26

He doesn't move another inch.

Time ticks by with every thundering pound of my pulse.

"Just tell me you want me," he whispers, so quietly I barely hear him. Closer, he tilts into me. His nose runs the length of my throat, coating my skin in hot fanning breaths. My core tightens when his mouth skims low along my collar bone. "Tell me what you desire, and it's yours." His teeth drag lightly across the top of my breast until my spine is arching into him desperately. "Just tell me you want my cock, love. Tell me you want me to fuck your pretty little cunt so deep, you'll do nothing but tremble beneath me and beg me for more." His magical fingers slide down my lips and throat as his mouth follows the path, and a violent volt of tingling energy pours into me from the small touch.

I want—I want him so fucking bad, I can feel it in every nerve of my body.

His hooded eyes meet mine once more. His lips hover over my parted gasping mouth. His tongue slides across his lower lip just before he speaks in the rumbling whisper once more. "Tell me—" dark lashes lift and a smile pulls at his lips, "tell me our thirty seconds are up, Ari. Tell me the rules are not meant to be broken." His head dips lower, and if I speak a single word, my lips will brush his. "Tell me, Ari," he taunts once more.

And it all clicks into place like rusty old gears turning.

He did this on purpose.

He doesn't want thirty seconds. He doesn't want rules. He isn't good with rules.

But this incubus very much needs hard lines.

27

Which is why we shouldn't be touching. If I let my guard down, if I let his craziness consume me, he'll never do what I'm about to ask him to do.

"Rules are rules, Krave." I pull back from him until my head hits the door with a quiet thud. "No touching," I say firmly, and it hurts my heart so damn bad, I swear we're going to hurt each other just being around one another.

He nod slowly. A look passes across his tragically handsome features, but he keeps on nodding. His hands release my thighs as his palms take their time skimming up my hips, my ribs, my breasts.

And then he isn't touching me at all.

With one step back, too much space presses between us.

Just like I said I wanted.

"Good," I say on a wavering tone. I slip out from beneath him, and when he can no longer see my reaction, I close my eyes hard and search for a full breath in my aching lungs. "I'm—I'm going to rest. Wake me when the sun goes down."

Another quiet nod.

I stand at the bed, and he still faces the door, unmoving.

"Krave," I say carefully. Remorsefully.

It takes time, but he brings his gaze to meet mine.

A painful beat passes between us.

"At dusk, I want you to take me to the cellar." My chin tilts high, forcing my composure once more as his brows lift in surprise.

I really don't know why he looks so stunned.

He and I both know I'll never leave the three men down there to rot.

CHAPTER FIVE
The Dungeon
Aries

A hot dampness assaults my nose the moment we take our first steps down the dark sloping tunnel. I'd like to say I'm not such a prissy princess that I've never wandered down into the depths of the castle's dungeons, but seriously, it smells like warm piss and lingering vomit, and I have never in my life stepped foot down here.

As a member of the Shadow Guard, I worked away from home. I had to separate myself from my kingdom if I wanted to help at all. I couldn't be caught. So I never once laid eyes on the demonic prisoners held within my own home.

"Just let me do all the talking when we get down there, love," Krave whispers, his hand hovering over the small of my back but not quite touching.

The way he doesn't touch me, it just seems to make me all the more aware of where his hands should be resting. Where his fingers would be grazing against my body. Where I should feel his tingling addicting touch.

Instead, I feel nothing but cold air between his long fingers and my prickling flesh.

The deeper down we go, the more the darkness settles in around us. Krave lifts his hand, and the sparkling smoke that clings to his fingertips shines little lights from the glinting silver glitter that's mixed with his dark magic. The white dim lighting dances along the wet brick walls. Literally. The shadows of a slender woman with a sweeping gown and a lithe man in a tailored suit sway intimately together, the flecks of silver meld together to create the little loving couple, and I do distinctly make out a detailed pair of curving horns arching up from her head. When the graceful man dips his partner with a bend of her slim figure, he places a chaste kiss to the center of her throat.

A shiver races down my neck.

I feel that kiss everywhere.

My attention slips to him, but he seems unaware of what artistic show his magic is performing for us. His attention is focused ahead, and I can't help but smile at him. The light carves his features into sharp lines and haunted beauty.

He's always so tragic-looking. So . . . tormented by the secrets he keeps.

He isn't a bad man. He's a good man in a bad, bad world.

And I'm tired of punishing him for the things we've

both done.

"Krave," I whisper, my fingers catching his for a single second.

Then he lifts that hand, shaking out and flicking away the pretty image of the couple like rain droplets from his hand. It's only then that I realize we've stopped walking. A cage-like door is in front of him, and through the thick bars, a pale face can be seen glaring back at us.

The guard on the other side has dirt streaked across his hard features. A deep scar runs through his right eyebrow and across his cheek. He seems like the type of guy who lives in a dungeon. Yes, he definitely looks like a dungeon master of sorts.

"Viral, how have you been? How is your . . ." the way Krave pauses, drawing out his dramatic flair with a wave of his hand, brings all attention to him. "How is your wife? Is she still as pretty as I remember?"

Wow. This . . . this is why I should let him do all the talking? Are you fucking kidding me right now? Viral's going to break everyone of Krave's long magical fingers one by one if he says another fucking word.

"She's well. Thank you, Mr. Salvation. We haven't forgotten what you've done for us." Viral's thick brows remain lowered over his dark eyes, but he nods to the incubus with total respect.

What. The. Demon. Fuck. Is happening right now?

"It was entirely my pleasure, Viral."

I blink dumbly at the two men. They ignore me and my gaping mouth entirely.

"My Princess was interested in purchasing a new demon or two. Are there any left after yesterday's auction?"

Krave is the most casual talker. He lies with ease. It shouldn't be an admirable trait, and yet in this moment, when I need through this locked door more than I need anything else in the world, it is a kind quality.

"Ah, the auction was canceled because of the rain. Rescheduled for tomorrow morning. I can't move anyone, but you're welcome to get an early glance at the stock, if you'd like." The way the guard says stock makes my stomach roil, and it makes me hate the man a little.

"That would be very appreciated." Krave nods with a charming smile. Disgust is still heavy in my throat. I can't force myself to mimic his politeness. My lips are pulled so far down, I'm sure misery and anger are written all across my face.

Clanking sounds scrape through the silence as the guard works the lock on his side. The incubus tilts his head, his inky hair falling into his eyes as he tips his head down to me. His touch sears across my arm as he trails his fingers lightly over my flesh. It's the briefest calming moment of his hands against my body.

"You're okay. Everything's going to be okay, Ari," he says on a quiet comforting whisper.

The door swings open. The warmth of his touch drops. In a matter of half a second, the façade that is Krave Salvation is right back in place.

"Thank you very much, Viral. Send my love to your wife," he says sincerely as he ushers me by on quick steps.

"I will. I will," the guard tells him with kindness now shining in his deep brown eyes.

What—

"What did you do for them? Did you fix some

erectile dysfunction? Tell him where the mysterious G-spot is? What did you do, Krave?"

He smirks as we pass waning torches along the brick wall. The tunnel continues down farther and farther.

And here I thought we were already in the dungeon . . .

"Is that all you think I'm good for, love? Fast fucks and hard cocks? That's all you think I know?"

When he passes me a sinful smile, I have to roll my eyes.

"His wife left him earlier this year. Said he was emotionally unavailable."

Yeah. I can see that being a thing for a guy named Viral.

"I caught him down here crying. Real tears. Big wailing man tears like I have never seen in all my centuries." Krave's smooth voice is perfect for fairytales and storytime. It makes warmth and sadness settle in my chest for the man who made me sick just moments ago. "I told him not to let her go. If he loved her, and he clearly did, don't let her go without showing her all he could be for her. Men get distracted easily. Jobs and money and stress all weigh them down, but they think they have to shield that stress away. Pretend to be strong and unyielding and just keep on going. Work harder to ignore it. When all women really want is their presence."

Oh. My. Fucking. Gods.

I'm in love with Krave Salvation.

Obviously, Catherine chirps from the back of my mind.

I stumble in the dim lighting. I almost fall face first

33

onto the piss-and-vomit brickwork. It takes everything in me to stagger awkwardly behind him as if I didn't just eat the ground because of how hard my heart's pounding from what he just said to me.

Don't let her go without showing her all he could be for her.

That's all Krave has been doing since the moment we met.

As I'm half jogging, half face-falling, he turns to me. He veers back with confusion crossing his smooth features.

"Are you alright? Is the smell getting to you? You look like you might be sick, love."

That's what love looks like for someone like me. Someone who has never let that warm and happy feeling hit their soul for even a heartbeat of a moment. Yeah, love looks like a godsdamn illness for people like me.

"I—I'm fine," I say as I swallow down the tension filling my throat. The longer I hold his gaze, the harder my heart pounds for me to cling to him, clutch him, kiss him, and whatever else Hallmark instructs women to do when they realize their heart isn't their own but shared with another.

"If you need me right now, just say the word. I'll promise to be quick if you promise to be quiet," he says with a wink.

Ah. Perfect. Just the blatant romantic words I need to clear my head before I do something really stupid.

"I'm good. Let's just find the others." I motion forward, but he studies me for a moment longer, like he knows exactly what I'm not saying.

Doubtful, but still. It's enough to make me nervous.

He lifts his palm, and once more hovers it at my lower back, leading me without ever touching me. My lashes close with a calm settling in to know we're fine. We're just as we always are.

Which isn't fine at all, if you think about it.

I shake my head and try to focus on the task at hand.

The tunnel slopes hard like a dirty slide before coming to level brick flooring. The room opens up to thick darkness and one single torch on the far wall, just near the barred cell.

Growls and hostile threats echo around the space, but one violent voice rings out to me among all others. "Fuck you! Fucking touch him again, and I'll shove my fist so far down your throat, your asshole will have a gag reflex."

"Zav, calm down. We don't want the guards down here again," Damien whispers, his palms planted on each of Zaviar's sweaty biceps as the angel glares pure rage at the other five men around them.

The others shift on their feet. Violence pulses like an organ pumping blood through the bricks of the walls surrounding them.

Whispers and slurs are spit their way, but no one dares to step toward the two men in the corner.

The ones who are so close to me, I could reach out and touch them. My heart aches with how near they are. It's a pain and a need, all at the same time.

My hands lift between the cold bars, and my fingers lightly kiss their skin. Dirt rolls beneath my fingertips, but I don't notice it. I'm too focused on how the tension eases from each of the two men's shoulders and wings. I know they feel me in a way that tells them exactly who I am with

35

just a single touch.

"Aries," Damien says on a catching whisper.

His dark wings shudder before he spins on his heels, and then he's looking down on me with big brown eyes. In a swoop of movement, he takes both of my hands in his and comes as close as the bars will let him as he drags his big hands over every inch of my body.

"I'm okay," I say slowly, but he's cradling my face in his hands and searches there as well, before his gaze slides from my lips to my eyes. His skin is hot to the touch as my fingers glide over his wrists. "I'm okay," I tell him once more.

A heavy breath slips from his lips and fans between us.

"You feel good," he whispers, like it's a painful admission to show his weakness in front of so many surrounding enemies. It makes me wrap myself around him as much as this fucking prison will allow and never let him go.

Tension presses from my chest and snaps between us as we cling to one another.

On the toes of my shoes, I arch against the cold cell, and ever so gently, I skim my lips against his. It's chaste. It's sentimental. But it doesn't stay that way. He tips my chin up even more, and I gasp against him as his tongue thrusts inside. Reverent strokes taste me deeply. It shoves aside my fears and wakes up my lust with a single demanding kiss from my sweet, not-so-innocent demon. My once-tender touch turns to clawing demanding nails that sink into his shoulders. He takes his time as the whispers begin to build around us.

"Seems the good little demon has found himself a piece of princess pussy," someone sneers.

Damien breaks the kiss and grabs his brother's arm tightly just as Zaviar lunges forward, scattering the other prisoners around them with a single lashing threat of violence.

Damien slams his brother back against the cell. Thick pink feathers slip out between the bars, and as I catch my breath, I make a mental note to possibly change his wings back to his holy white ones.

Unfortunately for him, magic is banished down here.

So . . . just try to keep that badass image intact for a bit longer, my frilly pink-feathered friend.

He's shaking, though. His fingers tremble against his palm. I know he's furious and in a constant state of threat here, but . . .

"Are you two sick?" My fingers slide around Zaviar's wrist, and just like his brother's, his skin is blazing hot to the touch.

Dirt streaks their faces, even in the dim lighting. Zaviar slowly slips out of my reach as his blue eyes shift around the room, like a predator taking inventory of his prey. "We're fine," he says gruffly.

"Infection is rampant down here." Krave's tone is low and quiet, but he's nearer than I realized. "Any minor scrape is a nice little home for the bacteria that suffocates the warm air in this place."

Dried blood covers their arms here and there. I try to think back to the night my brother died, but through all the memories of the blood, I can't remember if they were brutally hurt by the guards. Or even me.

Clearly, they were . . .

My heart sinks.

"I'm going to get you two out of here." I turn to the incubus at my side with wide eyes and rushing thoughts. "Krave, get Viral. Tell him—tell him—"

Long tingling fingers catch mine. "Ari, that's . . . that's not possible, love." The hurt in his black eyes is as palpable as the hurt slicing open my chest. "The king's magic controls this cell. And only the king's magic can open it."

The walls press in on me. His words break me down, and the little hope I had left, until my knees shake like they might give out right beneath me.

"Where's Ryke?" I blurt so loud that the question echoes up the bricks and around the dark ceiling.

I don't look up, but I'm faintly aware of the look Damien passes to his brother.

"Gravier took him earlier today," Damien finally says.

And I swear my heart stops dead in my chest.

My fucking father sat at lunch with me today.

All while these men grew sicker and sicker.

And the king plotted Ryke's punishment.

Or possibly, his death.

CHAPTER SIX
Ryke's Handler
Aries

My hands slam down on the long table, and the asshole seated across from me is not the one I want to take my anger out on, but he's the only one available at this late hour.

"Where the fuck is he?" I demand so loudly that the other men milling about flinch away from me and my temper tantrum.

"Easy A. You know if I knew, I'd tell you," Sev says with such a shit-eating smile, I don't believe him for a single fucking second.

"Easy A?" Krave repeats with a glare toward the Shadow Guard leaned back in his chair, his dirty boots kicked up on the paperwork littering the tabletop. "My apologies, who the fuck are you again?" Krave asks with all kindness but blatantly repressed hostility.

The other dozen or so men dressed in all black keep pretending to work on their files and their cases, but I'm very much aware that they're listening to every word passed within their range of hearing. It's their job, after all. They're alert. They're good at going unseen. And they're ruthless at getting information. And that's how I know that Sev knows.

"Tell me," I grind out, my teeth clenching so hard, my molars shoot a pain deep into my jaw.

"No," Sev says with a lift of his dark eyebrows. "Don't think that after three fucking years of radio silence you can prance in here with the king's pet on your leash and think for a single godsdamn second that I'll say *any*thing." His smile fades. "Your recklessness used to be inspiring. Now it's just dangerous. Get out. Before you fuck us all, like you did back in the necropolis the night you left."

There's a deadness in his eyes. That boyish charm of his is gone entirely, and for a moment, I don't know what to say to him.

But thankfully, someone else does.

"Get your dick out of your ass, and stop being a cunt to her." A small woman with long glossy red hair stops to look up from her manila folder. Her shifting gaze searches me like she's reading a book. "Gravier took the largest demon from the dungeon to gift him to his niece. He's too much of a racist fucker to realize it's the one he accused of killing his son. Bet they all look the same to him, you know?" She cocks a sharp eyebrow at me, and I can tell she's still trying to decide if I'm trustworthy or not.

I wonder if that's why she said what she did in such a harsh way. Or maybe that's her normal speaking voice . . .

"Thank you," I say, while my heart drops through my stomach.

He gave Ryke to Pen. Pen owns Ryke. Ryke's hers. And no matter how differently I say it, each time, it stabs through me over and over again.

He's bound to her.

I swallow hard.

"He was standing watch outside her bedroom door on the second floor just ten minutes ago," the pretty redhead adds as she knocks over a towering stack of papers to the floor. They flit around at her feet and I'm stunned to see Sev rushing to pick up after her. Her eyes close slowly with a breath pushing from her lips as if she isn't as put together as she seems on the surface.

I nod and turn toward the door.

"Be careful, Princess," she says on a rush. "He's a new one. They'll test him, you know?" Her head tilts low like she's back to reading her assignment, but I know she's still aware of me.

I was once the only female in the entire Shadow Guard. And now she is.

It's hard being surrounded by men twice your size while trying to carry your own.

She does it well.

"What's your name?" I finally ask as my palm slips over the cold metal door handle.

She continues to scan her papers. Seconds pass as if she didn't hear me at all.

And then, "Isabella," she says surprisingly.

A few men snort with covered laughter, like her pretty name and her pretty face are amusing to them.

But I do see the way Sev hasn't looked away from her since the moment she told him to get his cock out of his ass.

The tension in the place, I swear.

They're just as fucked as I remember.

***

I'm quiet as my fingers roam over the carved roses along the glossy banister. The incubus behind me whistles a tune like he doesn't have one fuck to spare in this world. I roll my eyes at him, and he just shrugs and keeps on with his flawless haunting melody.

I step up to the soft red rug on the second floor, and I peer to the left and then the right.

And there, hunched down on the floor, sits a demon. His big hands are thrown over his knees, and he looks so beaten down and defeated that my heart crumbles in my chest.

Anger flares up within me.

I swallow hard and go right to him.

The man who's been my shadow through all of this stays put, settling his lean frame against the wall as he watches me walk away.

My gown bunches around my legs as I fall with a quiet thud in front of Ryke. His head wobbles a little when he looks up at me from beneath his thick dark lashes. He smiles, but he winces when the pressure of it touches his eye that's swollen shut.

A deep split splices his lower lip so deeply, it cuts into me just looking at him.

Those fucking men who hurt him.

They'll pay. The guards. My father. All of them

signed their death warrant the moment they laid hands on this sweet, sweet man.

"Hey, Crow," he says with a coughing laugh. His head sinks down as he shakes from the pain I know he's holding back from me.

His warmth is overwhelming as I take his big hand in both of mine. He comes closer, and I lean into him as he rests his head against my shoulder.

"I'm so fucking sorry, Ryke. I tried to tell them. I tried—"

"Shhhh," he whispers, sliding his free hand along my arm and sinking it through my thick silver hair. "I'm fine. Don't think about that right now. Just be here with me for a little while. Please. Please stay here with me. Please, baby." His voice cracks, and my heart cracks right along with it.

What did they do to him in the dungeon? What happened after they took him away from me?

"I'm here." My words catch, and the tremble in my chest is a deeper feeling. It's something that isn't in my lungs or my flesh.

It's in my soul itself.

His hold on my hair tightens, and I love the sting of it even as he lifts my head up to him. His deep green eyes peer down on me from beneath the violence that's been done to his face.

And then his lips ghost over mine.

"Aries," he whispers against my lips.

My eyes close.

His breath warms my skin.

I tilt my chin up just slightly.

Just as the distinct sound of hinges swinging open

cuts through the thick silence.

I pull back from him, and he releases his hold immediately. It doesn't change the fact that I'm practically a heap of heavy-breathing hormones in his lap.

My attention lifts to find my cousin staring curiously down on us. Her hand clutches the white robe wrapped around her petite frame.

"Aries?" she asks with confusion heavy in her tone.

My gaze passes from her to the demon in front of me a few times before a thought finally stumbles forward in my cloudy brain.

"Your demon. He's sick. That shithole down there is a breeding site for infection, and it's demons like this who make our fine guard look bad. Take him to the infirmary. Now!" I stand and start to walk away without looking back at him.

Don't look back. Don't look back. Don't look back.

"The infirmary doesn't open until sunrise," Pen says.

I spin on the toes of my shoes, and it's really just an excuse to get one more glimpse of him. He's massive and strong, and yet, beaten and bruised.

He begged me to stay. And now I'm walking away.

And for what? The sake of an appearance? To make sure no one thinks I care for the monster they've painted this beautiful man to be?

I can't stay. Not now. But I can make sure he's taken care of.

"Then wake them. You are the Duchess of Roses. Wake. Them. The. Fuck. Up. Now, Pen!" My voice rakes down the quiet hall, and I hear feet shuffle behind closed doors like we have more of an audience than we can see.

But I don't care.

Pen nods so hard, I swear her pretty little blonde curls are going to come loose.

When she starts ushering Ryke to his feet, I turn away from them. Pain strikes through me to walk away.

But I do walk away from him.

For my sake, as well as his.

CHAPTER SEVEN
Mind, Body, and Soul
Zaviar

No one talks about it. Krave never once fucking talked about how you become a bound demon. Let me tell you a little story.

The King, the great and mighty King of Roses, fucking date-raped my ass into swearing myself to him. I was drugged. And beaten. And then I was intimately granted a temporary binding of quick spoken words. Bound heart and soul to some fucker who can't tell the difference between a demon and godsdamn seraph.

My jaw grinds as I stand on the wooden platform above the watchful fae. Damien stands at my side, the sunlight beaming down on his dirty golden skin and reminding me that he's more of a saint than I'll ever be.

I got him into this.

And eventually, I'll get him out of all of this.

It just won't be today.

"Yes, yes, gather round. Got your sights set on anyone in particular?" The little elderly woman asks a sniveling thin man at the very front.

He wipes his nose on the back of his hand as his beady eyes shift over the seven demons standing above him.

"Are—are any of them—p-p-pleasure demons?" The cocksucker asks on a squeak of a voice.

My lip curls back as I stand here. Every muscle in my body roars to lash out at him.

But powerful magic binds me in place. All I can do is stand still, glued to this spot. Even my voice is not my own in this moment. It's his. And he's willed it to shut the fuck up until I get my permanent bindings.

The clustered sound of too many people in one place rumbles around the little courtyard this fucking auction has been set up in on the east side of the castle. Guess they wanted good sunlight to show off their fucking pets in.

I shiver hard from the fever pounding through my skull. They didn't want to take the time to heal us. We'll be someone else's problem soon enough.

"Okay, quiet down. Quiet down and the auction will begin," the woman yells with a piercing pitch that causes my eye to twitch.

"First up, we have a fine, hardworking creature. Good laborer. Perfect for farm work or heavy lifting," the dark-haired little woman says as she motions to the first demon at the far side of the stage.

I'm last.

Damien will go before me.

And then . . . we might be split up.

A slamming feeling pounds through my chest, and I keep my eyes trained straight ahead. I mentally calculate how many attendees there are here. A hundred. Maybe a hundred and fifty. Some of them are clearly just fucking gawkers not looking to buy at all.

But the odds that we'll be bought by the same person . . . it doesn't look good for us.

"Next up, we have a smaller one. On the smaller side but still a good buy. Perfect for household chores or just personal use," the woman tells the crowd. The way she says *personal use* sets a tightness in my throat that feels a little like rage and bile all mixed into one.

Sweat clings to my temples, and it pours off of me the longer the auction carries on. One by one, bidders call out to bind their everlasting souls to the demons standing at my side. In sickness and in health. Until death do they part.

And then, Damien's next.

"This one's easy on the eyes. On the dirty side, but nothing a nice hot bath couldn't clean up, am I right, ladies? Those arms are made for lifting. Definitely an indoor or outdoor use for this one."

I'm going to be sick. I'm going to chuck chunks all over this fucking woman's glittering white shoes, and then I'm going to pray to the gods above to remember I fuckin' exist and that our power has got to be stronger than some fucked-up demon-fae bindings.

"What do you say? A hundred crowns to your king? Do I hear one hundred?"

"A hundred," someone calls from the back.

"One-ten," someone yells.

"Two hundred," Someone else says with a voice of confident finality.

"Oh . . . Well, someone wants that heavy lifting, it sounds like," the auctioneer says with a wag of her dark eyebrows. "Two-ten, anyone?"

"Two-ten," a woman in a fine gown and big blonde wings says with a wave of her elegant hand. Gemstones glitter from her fingers as she eats up the sight of my brother where he stands above her.

"Five hundred crowns and please move on," the familiar voice calls.

Whispers scuttle through the crowd, and even I try to catch a glimpse of the cocky woman. My lips curve in a slow smile as she steps slowly forward. Long silver hair fans across her big black wings, and she makes no effort to pull them fully in against her back as she passes the other attendees.

Aries.

I can't explain the way my heart soars like it's suddenly grown wings of its own.

She comes to the rich bitch's side, and she looks her dead in the face.

"Princess," Rich Bitch says. "I had no idea you participated in this kind of thing."

Aries presses her delicate fingers over her navy gown, and I'm mesmerized by the way it hugs her body. I don't know if I've ever seen someone so angelic look so sinfully bad before.

Aries tips her head up to the old woman at Damien's side. "Call the auction on this one. He's mine." She gives that command with all the power of a royal woman.

And all the claim of a demanding mate.

"Of course, Princess," the old woman says with a hurried nod. "Sold to Princess Aries for five hundred crowns."

The auctioneer tags Damien like they do cattle. Literally she sticks a silver pin right into the flesh of his shoulder and waves him toward the stairs on the right side of the stage.

Damien's eyes close but he doesn't make a sound as he stiffly walks off.

And then it's just me.

"Lastly, we have a pretty demon. Beautiful pink wings like I've never seen before," the woman says. Aries smiles big and wide at me, and if I could move, I'd give her cocky smile the middle finger right now. "He'd make a lovely maid, don't you think? Maybe a fashion advisor? I bet he has great taste in gowns, ladies."

Oh, the flattery goes on and fuckin' on. All the while, Princess fucking cocky pants down there laughs her tight little ass off at my expense.

"Do I hear one hundred crowns?"

"I'll give a hundred for the missus," a man with a thick accent says.

"One-fifty," a woman calls.

"Two hundred," another says with a giggle that, for some reason, sets me more on edge.

Fucking pink wings.

"T-t-t-two-ten." That voice echoes in my mind, and my gaze cuts right to the cocksucker from earlier.

My lip curls back as I recall what he was looking for. Fuck no.

My gaze falls hard to the silent princess in front of me.

She lifts her hand and studies her nails, picking at them like her manicure is the most important thing she should be worrying about right now, instead of my fucking asshole that's being threatened by the mousy bastard to her left.

More bids pass her by, and now she's flat-out gossiping with the rich bitch at her side. "Oh, I did hear that Betty Jean got engaged," Aries tells her with a rattling nod of her empty fuckin' head.

It's like she's fucking forgotten all about me.

What. The. Fuck.

My jaw shoots pain through my skull from how hard I'm grinding my teeth. I can't fucking talk. I can't fucking move. I can only stare at her.

While she ignores me completely.

"T-t-three hundred crowns!" Cocksucker calls out, his pale claw-like hand shooting high into the air.

Silence follows.

The elderly fae woman at my side shifts a little. Waiting.

Waiting.

Waiting.

"Oh. Uh, I don't know, like three-oh-five-ish. I think I have some change in my bra, just a sec," Aries says as she peeks down into her fucking cleavage.

What. The. Fuck!

"Yeah, let's do three-oh-five." She nods to the auctioneer, and the woman smiles nervously as she looks from Aries to the beady-eyed fuck and then back again.

"We normally do bids by tens, Princess. It would be three-ten," the woman says on a whisper.

"*Ohhhh*," Aries gives this tight-lipped back-and-forth shake of her head, as if that last five fuckin' crowns are really pressing her royal budget.

She gives me another once-over while I glare a hole through her pretty little empty head.

"Yeah. Uh. I guess—I guess that'll be fine."

"Perfect!" A sharp pin jams into my shoulder, and as I'm waved off the stage, I mouth Aries my thanks in the form of *I Hate You*.

She smirks at me, and when she blows me a fuck-you-too kiss, my heart skips a beat. I nearly choke as I swallow down the strange feelings. I meet Damien at the base of the stage, and he smiles at me like he, too, enjoyed Aries's little performance.

The assholes.

A large fae man with a silver name tag that reads *Cardence* is speaking in quick fast words over a demon and a fae, but I barely pay any attention to him as Aries casually strides toward us. She smiles and shakes hands with nearly everyone she passes.

She's here for us, but it seems she cares for them, too. Her people, they adore her.

It's not hard to believe. She's a beautiful woman. A powerful princess. A sexy fucking . . .

"I kind of feel bad for not letting that guy have you. He seems really upset," she tells me as she peers back at the mousy cocksucker still watching me.

Scratch all the kind things I just said about her.

She's a brat.

53

Always has been.

"You three are my last. Let's go," the large man, Cardence, calls to us. When he lifts his attention and realizes who he's yelling at, he changes his tune. "Oh. Princess Aries, I didn't recognize you. You're as radiant as I remember." His gaze drags over her body as he stares at her with a sort of starstruck admiration.

"Thank you. Are you performing the bindings today for my father, Cardence?" she asks him on an all-too-sweet voice. It's like an angelic melody. I don't even know who that voice is.

"Yes, I've been his binder for the last two years or so."

"Great!" She holds her hand out, and before either of us reacts, she takes Damien's hand in hers.

I don't know what they're doing. The temporary binding was just a quick spell of fast-spoken words that all blurred together in my dazed state. I don't remember holding the fae king's hand, though . . .

My brother's gaze is locked on her with a sudden seriousness. I've never seen him look so lost and found all at the same damn time.

Is that what love fuckin' looks like?

Does he love her?

My distracted thoughts slip away as Cardence's meaty hand carefully takes theirs. He turns their wrists until Damien's knuckles are facing him, and Aries's small hand is hidden beneath my brother's large one.

A long sharp pin lifts in the sunlight. Cardence holds it like a dagger instead of a thin little slice of metal. "I bind thee in magic. I bind thee blood. I bind your mind, your body, and your soul. Until death do thee part."

Fuck that's ominous.

Then he jams the pin right through the back of Damien's hand and into Aries's.

What the fuck.

Damien's shoulders tense. His jaw steels.

He doesn't make a fucking sound.

While Aries's lips part with a gasping pain that I've never heard her make before. She breathes through it in cutting breaths. Her lashes flutter over and over again, and still that fucking cock nugget, Cardence, just keeps the pin in place, lodged in their fucking flesh.

"Just a bit longer, Princess. Gotta let the blood intertwine," he mumbles.

Her lip trembles, and that's my undoing.

I'm behind her in an instant. My hands clasp over her hips, and she sags into me when my chest barely brushes her back. Long silver hair teases my lips. Smooth, perfect skin is beneath my palms. And then her free hand is over mine. It's a vice grip capable of crumbling every bone in my fingers.

And I let her.

"You're okay, Crow." I breathe the words without sound. I have no voice. But she understands.

She nods to me.

I hold her tighter.

She clings to my hand like she'll never let me go.

Why the fuck do I like it?

"And done," Fae Fuck Cardence says with an elaborate pull of his sharp pin. He slides it from their hands, and the very second she's free, she turns to me and wraps her lithe body all against mine.

My heart drops like a stone into a boiling deadly cauldron.

Then my palms push down her back, and I feel every heartbeat in her chest. I hear every cutting breath in her lungs. I . . . I have all of her vulnerabilities in the palms of my hands.

I've never felt her like this before.

She's never let me.

"Uh . . . alright. One more, correct?" Cardence interrupts, his sweaty fat head turning from her to me, and then back again.

Aries nods, her silver hair jarring against her small frame as she steps back from me. She releases me until only my hand is held in hers. Deep red blood slides over her knuckles and against my palm, but I never look away from her damp eyes.

She has to do it again.

Because of me.

I'm not even a demon. Some pretty little fae magic is really supposed to bind a seraph to a fae?

Doubtful.

We're just putting her through more pain for no reason. But she won't tell them my secret. And I have to keep that secret until my brother's future is figured out.

Whenever the fuck that might be.

"I bind thee in magic. I bind thee blood. I bind your mind, your body, and your soul. Until death do thee part," Cardence says on a bored, tired tone.

The threads I feel connecting me to the king fray. I feel them slip away like bindings that allow me my own voice once more. The pin slices through my skin like a blade blessed by the gods, and when it settles fully in, an unimaginable pain cuts through my heart.

"Fuck!" Deeper the agony pierces my soul, and in a matter of a single heartbeat, I realize this is much more than just physical pain that Aries and Damien were experiencing.

And they handled it a bit better than I am.

"Son of a cock fucker!" I growl out before grinding my teeth together so hard I taste enamel.

A shaking laugh slips from Aries's lips as tears stream down her smiling face.

The tiniest of smirks creases Cardence's lips, and I lash out. My free hand clutches his throat, and fear snaps into place across his features as my nails sink deeply into his flesh. He never releases our hands.

"Zaviar," Aries whispers.

Heat burns in my soul. It singes my veins. It scalds my flesh. Every part of me is on fucking fire.

Then the pin is pulled away.

The heat dulls. The pain retreats, and I finally release the man until he's doubled over and gasping for air that I hope burns the fuck out of his lungs.

I'm still glaring down on him and wishing him ill will when her small hands push across my pecs. The wound against her palm is already healed. That's the first thing I notice. The second is how fucking intense her eyes look. How pure her skin seems. How completely flawless she is.

She's . . . always been pretty.

But now, it's like everything about her has intensified.

My heart pulls, and all I want is to hold her again.

Her delicate hand lifts in the air. For a moment, I think she might cradle my head in her palm.

Then she whacks her hand against my dark hair.

"What are you thinking?" She hisses at me like an angry cat, and I feel so fucking dumbfounded. She just cursed my ass out, and I'm still puppy-dog eyeing her. What the fuck is wrong with me?

Maybe it'll wear off. Maybe I've lost too much blood, I'm too sick, I actually passed out, and this is all just a weird fucking dream my subconscious is feeding me because I've checked out her rack one too many times . . .

"Are you listening to me?" she shrieks. "Never, never touch a high fae!" She stops wagging her long finger at me long enough to turn to Cardence Fuckington. "I am so sorry, Cardence. Please accept my apology on behalf of my creature." She helps him stand to his full height, and though he glares hate messages at me, he wipes that look right off his face when he looks to her.

"Of course, Princess. It was nothing. These things," one more scathing glance my way, "*happen*."

He's stumbling away from us without another word and good fucking riddance for that.

Warm hands push over my chest once more. "Are you okay? You're pale." Then she does brush her hand over my cheek. "I'm sorry," she whispers, and it sounds like tragic romance lacing her words. "I brought you medicine from the infirmary." She pulls two small glass vials from within the fabric of her gown.

We each swallow down the bland-tasting liquid.

"*Are you* okay? You haven't said shit since the binding. Did it even work?" Damien asks, his brows pulled

58

low over his gentle eyes.

It takes me a minute to nod to the two of them. I nod harder, and I force myself to say something. Anything.

"Yeah. I'm fine. And I don't know if it worked."

My brother cocks a brow at me skeptically when I continue to avoid Aries's searching gaze. She's right in front of me. Touching me. Soothing me.

And I'm doing my best to ignore how intoxicating her touch feels.

"You don't know? Because my heart feels full. It feels bound, and I honestly hope it never goes back to how it felt before," Damien says with his eyes locked on her, and in return, she smiles softly to him.

An odd pain slices through my heart. I'm going to be sick.

I'm going to vomit all this fae magic up, and then I'll be fine.

I fucking have to.

Because the gods will never let me stay here.

Even if my mind, body, and soul belong to her now.

CHAPTER EIGHT
Her Demons
Aries

The two of them sleep off their fever in my bed. Not sending them down to the demon sleep quarters has really set off an array of whispering gossip around me.

I don't care.

I don't care about anything now. Because they're all safe. Even Ryke. Even if he isn't mine.

Now, it's time for the next step. The one I've actually been dreading . . .

I uncurl myself from the white chair in the corner of the bedroom and pull on black jeans and a black tee-shirt: standard Shadow Guard attire. I stare down at my clothes for a long moment before pulling the dagger from the back of my closet.

The same one I brought here the night I snuck into this room to kill *him*.

Can I really do that to my father? Can I kill the man who raised me and protected me?

He's cruel, arrogant, and entirely racist.

But he did protect me.

Especially from Nathiale . . .

I shove aside the conflicting emotions inside me and slide the dagger into my black boot. As I stride to the door, an incubus judges me from the corner of the room.

"You're really going to do it?" he asks quietly.

I nod.

He mirrors the motion.

"Do you want me to come?" Krave's so serious, it's alarming.

I shake my head at him, unable to admit in any way what I'm about to do.

He stares at me with white moonlight shining in his eyes. "Be careful, love," he whispers.

And those words follow me in my mind over and over again as I make my way to the highest tower.

To my father's bedchamber.

The thick shadows absorb my every move as I walk swiftly up the stairs, past the two guards, past my mother's room, and finally stand before the enormous curving door.

The coldness of the handle stings against my palm as I turn the knob. I ease the door open without a sound. The sleek red rug silences my steps and my gaze falls on the glossy wooden bedframe at the center of the room.

Candlelight flickers over the faint lines along his closed eyes. His long gray hair is fanned over the pillow, and the white shirt that he wears doesn't hug his broad shoulders the way his button-downs normally do.

There's no anger twisting his features. The skin along his face is thin and carves out the bones of his cheeks and brow.

He looks . . . *old*.

He's an old man clinging to old ways of life.

He's my father.

And I'm his daughter, standing with a knife held numbly in my hand. It isn't a weapon at all any more. It's just one more thing weighing down my body in this moment.

Right along with all my clashing emotions.

Don't, Catherine whispers faintly at the back of my mind.

I stay there for a long time. I stay until the candle finally burns out, leaving the large room in total darkness.

And in the darkness, I leave him.

***

"I heard she hugged him. Her demon. In the middle of the courtyard," Lady Lissia whispers from behind the back of her hand.

The two ladies-in-waiting make my bed while I linger just outside the door.

I don't care. Not really.

Why would I care?

"Oh, well, I heard she's fucking him. She's always been attracted to monsters, you know? Daddy issues, that one," Lady Castilla replies with a roll of her deep brown eyes.

My young cousin huffs a sigh at my side before squarely striding past me and right through the open door to my bedroom.

"That's funny, because I heard it was all none of your business." Pen folds her arms hard across her chest and looks the two ladies up and down. "If I hear another ill word against the future Queen of Roses, you'll both be shoveling horse shit for the next five years." She tips her chin up and both women mumble apologies before scurrying back to work with the large white bed sheet.

Ryke peers at me from the corner of his bruised eye, and we just stand there in stunned silence together.

I cannot believe she said that.

Her long red dress swishes out into the hall where I stand, and she tilts her head at me.

"You don't have to take care of me, Pen." My arm brushes against Ryke's when I pass him by, and that warm feeling of pain and pleasure sears across my flesh.

A tremble races down my spine, but I blink past the pleasant feeling.

"Someone needs to. Never let them speak like that. One harsh word can feed so many. And those who feed on ugliness only regurgitate that nastiness in tenfold."

Who is this woman? She was a little girl last time I was at court.

But clearly, she's learned how this kingdom works while I was off drinking myself stupid.

You can say that again, Catherine whispers.

Another shiver runs through me, but this time, it's a thing of surprise. I hear her less and less now days. I used to have to shove her away in the worst possible ways, and now . . . it's like she and I are one and the same.

"Your father wants me to help your image." She

doesn't even look at me as she says it. Her delicate features are focused straight ahead toward the long dimly-lit hall.

"Gods, of course he does." I bite my tongue before I say anything more, and it forces us to stay silent as we trail down the glossy staircase.

I stand there at the bottom of the stairs as men haul in bouquets of red roses large enough to crush them beneath their vases. But the dozens of men never stop moving, carrying in vase after vase into the ball room.

"Is the party tonight?" I ask quietly.

She nods, and I find her face turned up, and she's watching Ryke while he's looking away.

"Did you really—did you really have sex with your demon?" Her tone is so quiet, it gets swept up in the endless footfalls clattering around us.

I arch an eyebrow at the young girl. She's eighteen. She's smart and beautiful.

And now she's looking at Ryke.

I swallow hard.

He isn't my mate. It shouldn't matter.

"I've slept with demons before. I've slept with lots of men, Penelopia." I tap my fingers lightly against the roses carved into the sleek wooden banister, but I feel his gaze on me.

I feel his gaze like I've felt his possessive hands on my body.

I don't know how many times I can swallow back the emotions bubbling up inside me.

"And demons, they . . ." She clears her throat lightly, and whatever it is she wants to ask me, it doesn't seem to have the nerve to crawl out of her pursed lips. "I'm going to check on the flowers," she says so loudly, and suddenly I flinch.

Her heels click across the floor fast and hard, and she's gone in a matter of seconds.

But Ryke lingers.

My lashes lift, and my stomach is a mess of chaos as my eyes meet his. Despite his bruises and scars, he's so damn handsome when he smiles at me.

"She wanted to know if we're different," he says on a low rasp.

That chaos turns to a riot of lust low in my stomach.

I lift my shoulders and shrug at him.

"And are we?" He leans in close, his big hands clamping over the banister and caging me in with the weight of his broad chest pressing against my thin dress.

My fingers slip between us, and I trace every line carved deep into his skin. Every rune and every scar is rough against my fingertips. The hard pounding of his heart is smooth, though. Strong and demanding.

That's exactly what Ryke is: strong and demanding.

"You were more than different," I say on a ghost of a whisper.

His head tips low, and his mouth is so close to mine, I can taste the iron on his breath. "How so, Pretty Crow?" A big hand slides low down my back, and the room is empty just long enough, he seems to have the demon balls to travel even lower, with his fingers digging into my ass, so, so close to my sex that I can't even think straight.

My breath shakes when my lips part to give him exactly what he wants. "You were rough. Demanding and in control, but gentle and sweet, as you fucked me so hard, I can still feel your cock thrusting deep into my pussy if I close my eyes." My hooded eyes burn lust right into his gaze as we both breathe in those delicious memories of mine.

The groan that growls out of him quiets as he slides his tongue across his lips.

A hardness presses against my lower stomach, and it takes everything in me not to find the nearest closet and repeat that night over and over again until the fading memory becomes my every living reality.

"Ryke! I need you," a voice calls from far off.

That's all it takes. He shoves off from the banister, adjusting his cock from over his jeans as he strides right out of the room to go to the woman he's bound to.

And I'm left breathless and watching him walk away.

CHAPTER NINE
A Deadly Party
Aries

A gown of pure red is tight and distracting against my breasts. How do I know it's distracting? Well . . .

"Zav, are you listening to me?" Damien throws his hands in the air from where he stands behind my high backed throne, and I don't have to look at them to know Zaviar is staring at my chest again.

Krave stands on my right in a surprisingly tailored black suit, and I feel his presence more than I see him. Because my gaze is trained straight ahead on my father, who speaks to the crowd who wear fine dresses and sleek suits. They're here to drink and dance, and he's giving a thirty-five-minute speech about the economy.

It's . . . super exciting, as you can imagine.

"Our weekly auctions have had less than subpar

turnouts the last two weeks. Perhaps it is because demons are not as in fashion as they once were, but as I always say, demons are irreplaceable to our society, and we covet the aid they give us."

The aid they give us. They do everything but wipe my father's ass most days. Who is he kidding?

"If we do not get our attendance records up, we will have to drop the auctions to once a month, and that will cause all the good ones to be purchased before anyone has a chance. And we don't want that, do we?" He looks sincerely out at his bored audience. Nods and murmurs of agreement follow, though.

As they always do.

But one thing is clear, things are changing here. Just like with the tight clothing of the human realm that's now everywhere in our kingdom, perhaps guilt and humanity also has become the new trend in our lives.

Less and less do I see leashes on the demons in our kingdoms. They walk side by side with their handlers ever since someone a few days ago asked why Princess Aries doesn't leash her demons.

"Because they are not animals," I had replied curtly.

And then my father cut that discussion immediately.

"I won't keep you from the festivities. My daughter is home. The future Queen of Roses is with us once more. Let us celebrate!"

And just like that, no one mentions the young Prince who once sat where I sit now.

My gaze instinctively pans to my mother with that thought. She still hasn't said a word to me. What is there to say? *I'm sorry? I'm sorry I killed your only son and made your life more miserable than it already was?*

A heavy sigh pushes from my lungs and just lightly, Krave's long tattooed fingers skim against my outer hand.

Old music of soft-stringed instruments sways its melody through the high-domed ballroom. The entrance door is just to the left of the royal platform, and my attention keeps pulling there, as if I could just leave here and never look back.

But I can't. So instead, I listen to the melody. The song whisks across my skin and through my body as I listen to the man's soft song of heartbreak and love.

It's definitely a trendy little topic of our lives now, isn't it?

We're seated just above everyone else on the platform, and its pretensious, but it makes for good spying at this level. Men and women dance across the shining white floor, but my gaze follows my father as he chats with his newest advisor. He's a younger man. The man smiling and nodding along with my father isn't the elder fae I remember hobbling along in my childhood.

The top of Nille's head bobs past my table, and I have to call out to the rushing goblin to get him to pause for even a second.

"Who is that man?" I motion discreetly to the blonde fae man at my father's side.

Nille's big eyes shift to the two of them. "Johnn Rarely. He's been the King's advisor for two years now. Only had his trust for one, of course." Nille shakes his big head at the man as he carries on past me to my mother's side.

He's young. That's the only thing about him that I keep thinking about.

He isn't old, and he doesn't harbor old ways of thinking.

I keep stewing on how Johnn Rarely can fit into my life and my plans when a rasping tone whispers in my ear like sex smothered in honey, "Stop suffocating on politics and dance with me, Ari," Krave says as he hovers near my side but keeps a nice, respectable distance between a handler and her demon.

My heart answers before my lips ever part with a breathless response.

His fingers slide into mine, and I stand. He guides me down the stairs and through the parting crowd, who watch us with far too much interest. If Krave were a fae—hell, if Krave were a goblin, he'd be getting less notice right now. But they stare at him, gawking openly, as he gracefully takes my hands and positions them with too much space between us.

Because they're watching him.

And I fucking hate them all for it.

My hands push over his smooth black suit that matches his eyes, and I press myself nice and close against his chest as my hands slide through his soft inky hair.

"That's better," I whisper along his cheek.

A taunting smile carves his lips and the way his beautiful dark eyes are shining down on me, I can tell he agrees. He's always made me crazy in the worst and best possible way.

I'm just starting to wonder if I've always done the same for him.

His shining black shoes glide over the floor as if he's danced this dance a thousand times. Almost as if . . . he's a royal gentleman.

If Krave stayed in the Torch, who would he be? I bet he'd have women, a few of them pawing all over him. Friends—I know he'd have friends. I've met Phoenix and the others, and I know they would take care of him. But instead, he's had a life of servitude. A life of cruelty.

"Why did you come here to the fae realm, Krave?" When the words gasp out of my mouth like a whispered accusation, his brows pull together as if it's the most obvious thing in all the realms.

My heart's pounding hard as if it, too, knows, and I'm the only stupid fool left wondering.

His head dips low, his smooth cheek brushing along mine before his mouth grazes over the outer shell of my ear in the most intimate way.

"Because my soul knew that my mate was here."

A shiver slides down my spine so fast, it takes over my entire body in a hard tremble that I can't hide.

My chin lifts, and he meets my searching gaze with a look of pure sincerity.

Long black fingers leave from my hip, and soon, he's tracing the curve of my jaw. And more shivers follow in the wake of that sweet, igniting touch.

"I came wandering into this little fae castle to find what my heart knew belonged to it. And I found your dear old daddy instead. The King beat me with a fire poker for breaking into his ill-guarded home. I told him he needed better security on the west wing, but did he listen to me?" His head shakes slightly with a roll of his big eyes. Before a seriousness overtakes his hauntingly handsome features. "He broke my hand." His fingers shake just slightly along my cheek. "I refused to leave, though. And the moment he said your name, the moment he whispered the sweetest words I'd never heard, I knew." The intent way his eyes are locked on mine demands me to be closer. My chest is pressed hard against his, and I have absolutely no idea how he's still leading us around the shining ballroom with how little space I'm giving him. "He lifted the metal rod high above his head, and I didn't flinch as the words *Aries Sinclaire* echoed through my brain over and over again." Smoke slips from his fingertip, and just faintly, the furious face of my father can be seen in the sheer inky colors of his magic.

My palm lifts, and I take his trembling hand in mine. He stares at our hands interlocked for a long moment, before a heavy breath pushes from his lungs, and he shakes the serious look away.

He covers it with a wide, fake smile that hurts my heart to look at.

"Why didn't he kill you, Krave?" It's my turn to brush my fingers beneath the metal piercing at the center of his lower lip. It shines beneath the golden light as his eyes dim with a memory I don't know if I want to hear or not.

"Because I said your sweet name right back to him. I said it over and over and over again. My mind was obsessed with the sound of your name. And then my magic was, too. Clouds of smoke drew every angle of your alluring features. The bow of your lip. The curve of your delicate neck. The warmth of your smile. It glittered around us, and I locked eyes with a woman I'd never met before. Someone my heart knew even if my mind never did. I remember thinking—" he swallows hard, shifting his attention away from me to the other dancers swirling around us. He pauses on my father standing at the back of the room, and the incubus's smile softens with genuine amusement. "I remember thinking, this intoxicatingly beautiful woman is going to get me killed someday."

My heart dips without a solid beat to support it.

My father knew Krave was my mate. He knew that he loved me. And he used that love against us.

Krave bound himself to a man who hated him, just to be near me. Soon, I hated the demon, too, for it. It never made him change his feelings about me, though. He never once stopped wanting me.

My arms cling tighter around his lithe frame, so tight he stops swaying through the crowd. We stand there, my face tucked into the crook of his neck as he just holds me. Gentle music carries on without us. Laughter and whispers surround us. None of it breaks through to the two of us. He simply holds me, and I hope he never ever lets me go.

"I love you, Krave." My voice cuts out with an uneven breath against his skin.

Long fingers slide beneath my chin until I'm looking up at the lost look in his eyes. His attention sweeps over the rawness of my features, the raggedness of the breaths parting my lips.

"And I have loved you since the moment I locked eyes with the smoky shadows of my own magic. It seems that, sometimes, the shadows love us back."

Sometimes the shadows love us back.

My heart breaks for him and pounds for him all at the same time. There's darkness between us. It'll always be there. We can't change that. But I love him more because of that darkness.

My heels angle forward, and I lift against him until my mouth almost brushes his. A sweet smile is against his lips as his head dips down to meet me halfway.

Then a booming voice cuts through the veil we've created around us.

"Friends, friends," my father calls out to his loyal subjects.

Krave pulls back from me just slightly, his eyes closing slowly.

Dear old daddy is still pushing us apart, it seems.

My head falls with my forehead resting against Krave's pressed black button-down. *Can this night just be over? Can we be done? What else is there to show off to these people that he hasn't already shown off before?*

"Have I forgotten to tell you about the main event?" My father asks, his voice carrying through the room of excited murmurs. I glance over to him, and his long silver hair shifts around him as he looks out at his people. Oddly, his gaze settles on me. "Tonight, we'll be having a battle. Right here. Among us. We will smell the sweat and taste the blood as if the fight is our own."

What. The. Fuck.

My attention snaps to Damien and Zaviar, but they're both safely standing behind the royal table on the platform, far enough from my father that they seem out of his reach but not far enough away that they seem protected.

My feet are stumbling over themselves as I push through the dumbstruck people staring at my demented father. I make it up the high standing royal platform and to the table with my heels wobbling beneath me, but I don't give a damn about composure. Even as my father's heavy gaze follows me every step of the way. In seconds, I'm at my throne, standing behind the tall chair, just in front of two innocent men. I shield them with my small frame as much as I can, but I know my father's mind is on them and them alone.

My attention cuts to a single, ancient weapon that glitters with opal stones along the hilt. I think it's more for decor. They call it the crowning sword, and it's only ever used for ceremonies to announce a new ruler.

But I'd still use it if I had to.

"I've recently acquired a very skilled warrior. In the nasty Torch, his own people, they call him the Demon Monster." A chuckle shakes through my father's wide chest as if he's just said the funniest fucking thing. His people laugh with him.

I do note that Johnn does not smile. Not once.

Interesting.

"Demon Monster is thirsty for a fight, and what do you say? Shall we give him one?" Cheers and applause trail after my father's question.

Fuck.

I'm still shaking my head at how completely ridiculous this all is when a man—nay—a fucking walking mountain strides in. He turns himself sideways to slide through the doorway without harming his flaking gray wings. They hang over his back like worn stone preparing to bury him where he stands. A deep scar cuts through his lip and cheek, revealing black teeth at the back of his jaw. I wince at that sight alone, but that isn't the worst of it. The big fists that hang at his sides have claws where his fingers should be. Thick gray claws hang just slightly too low on his big arms. The echo of his heavy footfalls storms the room, and the once-happy partygoers, the ones who cheered for this Demon Monster to make his appearance, are now scattered back as close to the wall as they can get.

"Demon Monster," my father says with more affection than I ever remember hearing in his tone.

The demon's tattered lip curls back, and he grunts in response.

Charming.

"Would anyone's demon care to entertain us with a fight to the death?" The King's attention sweeps the crowd slowly, but I know he's coming my way.

I know what he wants.

And he can't fucking have either one of them. My shoulders square as my chin lifts obnoxiously high. I'll just tell him. I'll tell my father to fuck right the fuck off. I will.

His scanning gaze stops abruptly at the center of the crowd.

On Krave.

My knotted stomach tumbles even lower as my breath lodges in my throat.

The King's smile widens with what appears to be affection as he looks at my mate. His lips part, and I just know he's about to volunteer him.

He doesn't own Krave anymore. He's mine to have and to hold. But an order from the King is still an order.

"I'd love the honor, my King," someone else says before Krave's name is uttered from my father's lips.

Murmurs crawl up from the fear that's thick in the air, and as I search over the elegant gowns and the fine suits,

I can't see who took the challenge against Demon Monster.

Who has the demon balls to fight someone who looks like someone the boogie man lost his virginity to and has been infatuated with ever since?

Ryke steps forward.

"No," I whisper like a plea.

All eyes are glued to the large demon. The runes scarring his chest are so deep, the skin is twisted in some places. Big black wings are held tight against his broad shoulders. Jagged iron cuts through his skin along each forearm, and I know he's strong. He's powerful and relentless.

If he loses, it won't be without a fight. And if he wins, he'll be the monster he always knew these people would turn him into.

Pen's lips are parted, and her eyes are like saucers as she watches her demon.

Dampness clings to my lashes when I blink hard and fast. He's watching me, holding his attention on me intently as he makes his way to the center of the ballroom.

Demon Monster eye-fucks Ryke like he's going to literally fuck him. And not in the good way.

He isn't mine. He isn't mine. He isn't mine.

I chant over and over and over again.

It's the truth.

But then, why does my heart feel like it's wide open and waiting to be cut to pieces?

Pen steps to the edge of the crowd, and her big eyes shine. Just like mine.

She's young. Young and about to have her heart shattered.

Just like mine.

"Stop!" My lips snap together fast but not fast enough to refrain from screaming that one little word out.

Johnn's attention shoots to me from where he stands just near the table. His eyebrows lift and he, like everyone else, waits for me to say more.

"Father," I have to be careful. He'll send me away to another realm entirely if I say the wrong thing. And then who will protect my men? "this room is much too small for a battle, don't you think?"

That's the best you have? Catherine huffs from the back of my mind.

"Shut up," I say under my breath, gaining me another interested look from Johnn.

"Nonsense. It's the perfect size, my dear," the King says with another smile.

"The room's too small!" I say once more with conviction and irritation lacing my words.

Stop fucking raising your brow at me, Johnn. Worry about your own fucking problems. Like who will rule this kingdom if I kill the King and run away to the demon realm to live happily ever after.

"Aries," my father warns.

"The room's just fine, Crow," Ryke says with a cocky smile.

Gods, why is he so damn cocky? Why? Why can't for once he just back away and say, "You know, this is too much. Maybe Demon Monster, Boogie Man Fucker is a bit too much for me."

Demon Monster prowls toward Ryke, and when they face off at the center of the white tile floor, it's apparent just how terrifyingly large Demon Monster is. From the tips of his taloned wings to the toes of his dirty boots, he's three times the size of Ryke.

"*Fu—ccckkk*," Zaviar whispers from behind me.

And I couldn't agree more.

"Gentlemen," my father says with big greedy eyes eating them up, "On my signal, you'll begin. The only rule is, only one monster will win. The other will die the most dishonorable of deaths. The loser will have disappointed not only me, but all the realms." My jaw clenches just as my nails bite into my palms so hard, I feel warm blood lick at my fingertips.

My father's hand lifts and falls with dramatic finality.

Demon Monster launches himself forward without hesitation. His ashen claws grip Ryke's biceps, and he slams him to the ground so hard that it rattles the crystals of the chandeliers above. It rattles my heart. Instead of pummeling him over and over and over again, the demon lets his claws sink with severity into the muscle of Ryke's arms.

A cry of agony tears from Ryke's throat and echoes around the room like a haunting melody. Wetness slides down my cheeks, but my jaws are locked tightly together without sound.

Ryke has little room to move beneath the enormous man. He thrusts his fist into Monster Demon's solid abdomen again and again but there just isn't space for impact.

It's a quiet struggle that's so silent, I can hear my own jagged breaths. It could end in seconds. Ryke's heart could slow before stopping suddenly.

The empty sound settles in.

And that's when he twists his wrist between them, and brings down his iron blade along his forearms, tearing through the demon's flesh with a deep gashing slice. Blood splatters over both of them. It coats the shining tiles.

Cheers and encouragement call through the room then. It's a riot of noise that demands my heart race faster as I watch with wide eyes.

A roar of anger and pain shakes through the room from Demon Monster's blackened mouth. Ryke lifts his foot and kicks the beast off of him, buying him space and time. He stands while the other demon continues to breathe through the agony of the deep wound across his colossal chest.

Ryke's boot comes up and thrusts down on the demon, planting him beneath his foot. "The harder they fall," Ryke whispers as he stares down at him.

It really does seem like it'll end fast and easy.

As Ryke's mossy green eyes glare down at the bloody man. And my sweet demon's features start to melt. His body twists and molds into a thin, curving figure that I don't understand. Scales ripple over his flesh. His eyes narrow into emerald slits. A slithering tongue hisses out from his mouth.

Ryke morphed into a snake . . . while also keeping the two-legged shape of a man.

Demon Monster shoves back against the slick flooring, putting space between him and the creature Ryke's magic has deemed the thing most feared.

Even if Demon Monster is the only one who recognizes that fear.

"Reptrilen," the demon says on a shuddering

whisper.

Does Ryke even know who Reptrillen is? I have no idea how his magic works. But it's terrifying. The things of nightmares.

Ryke tilts his scaly head slowly to the side. In the blink of an eye, the snake lashes out. And his fangs sink deeply into the demon's throat.

It's a quick strike. A fatal one.

When Ryke pulls back, his jawbone returns, his beard rapidly grows dark over the thin scars lining his features. And then, he's entirely himself again.

But he continues to keep his attention fixed hard on the man who now lies poisoned and bleeding out at his feet.

Demon Monster's big body shakes just slightly. It's an odd sight. I don't understand it. Until . . . laughter slips from his tattered lips.

"You fool," the demon says on an accented growl of words. "You know what I am?" His head tips back, and he lies there as if he's preparing for a nap. "Bet you never been to the Torch or the Ash Empire." The demon settles Ryke with a look of cruelty. His lip curls even more. "Our Ash is a poison, you stupid fuck." He lifts his clawed gray hand, and it clicks for me at the same time as it clicks for Ryke.

Ryke's knees wobble beneath him, and he stumbles back. Gray bruises cover his upper arms around the dark claw marks branding his skin.

"No," I whisper once more, but there's no breath in my lungs to carry the sentiment.

Veins turn gray beneath the surface of Ryke's scarred skin. They shatter up his arms, across his throat and kiss along his lips. Still he stands tall, wavering just slightly as he faces his opponent head on.

Demon Monster shakes his head at him as he shoves to his feet and slowly circles Ryke. It's a drawn-out taunting as though he's waiting for the man to just drop dead where he stands.

But that's not Ryke's style.

He storms forward with deadly intent. With only a few feet separating them, his wings lash out from his back, and he swoops down on the demon from a high striking point. His elbow crashes hard against a cracking nose, and the slice of flesh follows the blow as his blade cuts across the demon's cheek, spraying blood from the wound onto the fine gowns of women standing too close.

His fist slaps over the wet blood on the man's face, and they both go tumbling down in a heap of violence and anger. Demon Monster flips them the moment they hit the floor, and his blood showers down on Ryke as they fumble against one another with lashing claws and striking blades. Gray nails sink into Ryke's throat. He growls a gargling sound and never slows his slamming fists against the man. Claws sink in. One at a time. Slow. Torturously slow. A smile carves across the monster's mouth.

He truly is a monster.

Air chokes along Ryke's lips. They turn blue among the gray. He looks ashen and dying. It's a nightmare I can't look away from.

Ryke's lips part wider for a breath that he can't have. His eyes grow big. Life fades from his eyes little by little.

He's so strong, he continues to fight even as his motions slow. He kicks. Punches. Everything he can do, he does.

It's just not enough.

And I know he knows it.

His jaw clamps shut, grinding hard with determination. He thrusts his arm straight up between them until his own fist is held near his throat. Then he slams his forearm into the demon's chest. A crack like bone snapping in two sounds through the room. Blood sprays down Ryke's arm around his black blade. He's shoved it in deep, and I can see the surprise on Demon Monster's face. That iron-like mouth opens with only a rattling gasp. That look only intensifies as Ryke brings his blade down hard, gutting the man from sternum to navel.

A breath cuts from the demon's lips. And then he falls into Ryke with the full weight of his corpse.

Crimson covers Ryke like a blanket. His wet hands shove at the monster until his body thumps against the floor at his side.

My feet are moving before my mind even processes it all. My red dress darkens at the hem as I slide over the mess covering the floor. I don't even think about it as I drop to my knees at his side.

His lips tremble when his gaze finds me.

He's so broken and victorious as he smiles at me.

"Told you the room was big enough, baby," he says on the weakest tone I've ever heard from him. My fingers tangle through the slickness of his own, and I can't think or speak as gray lines crawl across his face.

"Help," I whisper before finding my voice on a shaking scream. "He—he needs help."

I look up to find fae in beautiful gowns and shining diamonds surrounding us from a safe distance. None of them with their many differing powers step forward to help us. I pause when I see Pen slumped on the floor with quiet tears streaming down her face. A few people meet my eyes, but most of them look at absolutely anything else. Krave watches Ryke with big black eyes, but there's nothing he can do.

Nothing.

No one will help him.

Steady hands reach out to me. I peer back to find someone I barely know knelt down in the blood at my side. Kind brown eyes meet mine.

"Excuse me," Johnn whispers with a small smile.

He—he wants to help . . .

I push back from Ryke, sliding against the floor to give the fae some room. Johnn's fingers skim over Ryke's neck, and it's an eerie sight not to react to.

He won't hurt him. I hope.

I don't want to trust him. It's just, I have no other options.

He's all I have.

White fumes billow up from the man's hands. He focuses on his work. His brows pull low as he puts more power into it, and even more fumes spread around them.

The gray poison beneath Ryke's throat fades. Pale skin replaces the strange dark lines, and soon he looks normal. Slow breathing, but normal.

Johnn releases a big breath before lowering his hands and settling back a few inches from his patient.

"Are you a healer?" I ask with disbelief.

Johnn shakes his head. He peers back at where my father's throne stands. He's being as careful as I always am.

But it's empty. My father is gone.

"I'm a tracker. I take the essence of something, and I can return it to where it's from. It allows me to track things and people. I returned the ash poison back to where it came from. That's what I did for your friend. I didn't heal him. He'll still need his wounds tended to." Johnn eases to his feet without another word.

He leaves us in a rush of rapid footfalls.

Because he knows he's in trouble.

We all are.

CHAPTER TEN
Cross the Line
Damien

She's vacant. I could see it in her eyes. I helped her lay Ryke down in the demon's chambers an hour ago, and I had to force her to go get cleaned up instead of waiting by his bedside or commanding Pen to get him better living quarters. Zaviar and Krave stayed, promising to look after him. But I couldn't.

I linger in her bedroom now. She told me to go, but I can't leave her.

Not like this.

Water drips with trickling sounds from the open bathroom door. I'm tempted to check on her but there's a fine line between being a friend and being a creep. I'm just on that side of the creep line right now as I hover at the bathroom door.

The scent of a warm water and lavender fill my nose. Still I wait.

She doesn't need me to wash her fucking hair.

She . . . she doesn't need me at all really. She's fearless and smart and . . .

Naked.

She steps out of the room without a towel. Without a single fucking shred of clothing.

And at some point, I have to remember to pick my jaw up off the ground from where I dropped it on the other side of that creep line.

She doesn't say anything as she passes me, her hips swaying with every perfect step she takes.

Gods her body—

Ryke's in pain. And she's worried about him. Now is not the time to think about how nice her tits look when they're wet.

I clear my throat hard and try not to stumble over my words when I speak. "Can I get you anything?"

Her wet silver hair shifts along her back as she shakes her head without glancing back at me. She opens her closet and picks out the first outfit her hands catch on. She slides a black shirt over her head and it wafts open in the back around her big black wings. I'm surprised when she leans forward for the black jeans in her hands. I almost comment on the Bin style clothes here at court, but then she starts shimmying into underwear and jeans, and the bounce of her ass in those thin lace panties distracts the thought right out of my head.

"Why are you getting dressed? It's late. You should

sleep."

"I have to meet someone," she says absently as she tugs on a pair of new black boots that stop just above her knee.

She looks like a sexy assassin ready to walk the cat walk and possibly slit a few throats along the way.

"Who?" I ask, but she's already headed toward the door. "Where are you going? Will you just hold on a second!" She doesn't stop.

Not until she swings the door open.

And there stands Krave, leaning against the doorjamb like he's been there for a good long while.

Seems I'm not the only creep toeing the line.

"Going somewhere, love?" he asks, a bit less desperately than I had.

He's dressed in dark jeans that fade into the darkness of the hallway, but his pale chest only makes him stand out even more against the shadows.

"What is with you two! I'm going to meet with the Shadow Guard," she hisses on a harsh whisper.

The Shadow Guard. Her secret team of friends. Right.

I should calm down.

She's not rushing out to murder her father for what he did tonight. She isn't a thoughtless killer. She's smarter than that. I'm blowing things out of proportion.

"You think Sev will help you discreetly kill your father?" Krave tilts his head at her, his messy black hair falling across his inky eyes.

Fuck. I was wrong. I was putting things exactly into the proportion they needed to be. Aries does want to kill her

91

father. And she'd be executed for that. The fae realm would never stand for the murder of a king who's ruled for the past two centuries.

My fingers lift, and her smooth skin brushes over my fingertips as I catch her wrist in my hand. She only glares back at me, gifting me with the same look she used to reserve for Krave.

My hand drops just like my stomach does.

Her features soften as she stares at me with the brightest silver eyes I've ever seen. I've never met someone so beautiful and so beaten down by the world they live in.

People think life is easier when you're pretty. As a once-perfectly-created seraph, I do understand that thought, but absolutely nothing in Aries's life is easy.

"I'm not going to kill my father," she whispers on an empty, defeated breath. The constant tormenting smile on Krave's face slowly fades, and I know he wants to wrap her up and never let the world hurt her ever again. "I do need to speak with the Shadow Guard, though." She squares her shoulders, and the second she takes a single step forward, Krave gets the hell out of her way.

Then the two of us are trailing after her in the dark.

Every nerve in my body is on edge as I follow her down the sleek staircase. A man is posted at the front door. He's stoic, and the princess doesn't give him an ounce of her royal attention as she glides past him and strides to the kitchen.

Moonlight shines in through the big windows. It gleams across the clean white counters. She walks through the empty, silent room. I arch a brow when she stops next to the towering oak cabinets and lifts her hands to the flat stone wall.

Her delicate fingers press gently on a stone.

And that stone shifts beneath her touch. They all do. The many bricks twist this way and that and scatter across the wall to make space.

It makes just enough of an opening for a small doorway to fit into the total enveloping blackness.

I swallow hard at the sight of the mysterious hidden door. When she walks forward, so does Krave. And so do I.

I have no idea where we're going.

I don't ask. It's not my job to ask. Right now, my job is to follow her.

And I'll follow after this beautiful, reckless woman right to the bowels of hell.

CHAPTER ELEVEN
Endurance
Aries

The guard are as busy as they always are at one in the morning. Sev and the woman I met earlier are both hovering over an untitled map with zero words written on it that might indicate where they're headed. Just landmarks.

The guard are cautious. Another thing they are is untrusting.

And Sev, he doesn't fucking trust me anymore.

"I think you're lost, Pretty Princess," he says, rolling up the map the moment he spots me standing among the rushed work flow of the other Shadow Guards. "Best get back to rest. Wouldn't want to disappoint Daddy by being late to another ball where a demon's slaughtered just for entertainment." His gray wings ruffle behind him as he folds his arms across his black shirt.

Isabella slowly passes him an annoyed look.

It's just what I'm counting on.

Everyone here wants me to fuck off because they think I'll get them all killed. But Isabella has faith in me.

For some bizarre reason.

"Isabella, do you have a minute?"

I note a man to her right stops flipping through his file folder to glance our way, passing me a look that tells me Sev isn't the only one who wants me to fuck off.

My heart beat drums in my chest as I wait for the small woman to speak. She's quiet, but she's really making this painful for me to stand here and be stared at by the people I once called my friends.

Shining red hair shifts along her soft features as Isabella nods. She doesn't say anything when she slips by me. She's headed to the office, and I pretend like I'm not completely unsure as I follow her back there.

We slip inside among the cluttered filing cabinets that no longer have the space to line the walls. I stand at the center of the angled cabinets with Isabella, and by the time Krave and Damien both come inside, there's no room for our wings. Isabella's feathers flutter along her back, scattering loose papers atop the cabinets but she calms and pulls them back in it seems. I shift on my feet until my big black wings fade away, settling inside myself like a comfortable blanket wrapping around me. Damien smiles slightly at the sight of my glamouring magic while Krave doesn't much notice at all.

He's used to it.

That and he's nearly as powerful as I am in some

ways, so I don't expect the same impressed glance from him.

But there's more room now, and that's all that matters.

My hand presses to the old wooden door, but as it starts to glide shut, a shining black boot kicks between the frame and the door.

Sev.

Perfect.

"We don't need you here for this, Sev," the woman says to him on that calm but annoyed tone of hers.

He pushes into the room, his wings brushing Krave's as they stand side by side. He closes the door behind him and looks up at us with a big smile. "I didn't ask if you needed me. You're my partner, and it's dangerous to be alone with the second-most-watched person in this kingdom."

My brow arches high. "I'm on your watch list?"

Sev's smirk spreads harder across his obnoxious face. "Did you think you weren't? After everything? After walking around with your dead brother's crown on your head? After binding two demons and an angel to your soul? After standing watch during a fucking homicide?" His voice grows louder and louder, but all my attention catches on is that one little word.

"You knew he was an angel?" My throat dries. My stomach twists.

If others know what Zaviar is, he's in danger. Not from us . . . but from the gods.

Sev shakes his head back and forth like he can't believe that's the one thing I have a problem with among all that other shit.

"What do you want, Aries?" His jaw grinds, and it's

hard for me to hear that tone in his voice.

Because before he was Isabella's partner, he was mine.

He was the brother I always wanted—yes, I'm not counting Nathiale. I never will.

He and I, we found this maid's room that was bricked over decades ago. We found this safe place for us and our friends who couldn't stand to see the world the way it was around us. We created the Shadow Guard.

And now, I'm not welcome here.

"I want to dethrone the King of Roses." My chin lifts, and I force the look of flawless confidence across my face as my wings quiver inside myself.

"Dethrone?" Sev says loud and spitefully. "We don't want him dethroned. We want him dead, Aries!"

"Why do you want to dethrone him?" Isabella asks more rationally.

"Because killing him will only incite centuries of war. If I'm crowned after his assassination, it will win me loyalty from people like us. But people like him, they'll never give us peace." I tell them all of this, and it's like an echo in my head now from how many times I've thought it through.

But Sev isn't nodding along like Isabella is.

He reaches for me, venomous words curling back his lips before he's even spoken, but he's cut off when someone grips his wrist hard enough to turn his hand white.

Damien steps closer, clenching the other man's hand so tightly that Sev's lips snap closed with a twisting look.

"Do not lay a fucking hand on her," the demon growls out. It's eerily like his brother, but his face isn't pained with hate. I know he means what he just said; he's just not filled with cruelty the way Zaviar is.

Sev jerks his hand away from Damien, the two of them holding gazes for far too long in such a small space that's not nearly big enough for all these masculine death glares. Meanwhile, Krave looks so damn happy. I can tell he's just waiting for a fist fight.

"I think you three should leave. We can't help you." Sev's words are flat and leave no room for argument.

I should have known better than to come back here. There's too much between me and the friends I once had.

He's right. I should leave.

I only take a single step when Isabella catches my hand. Her long lashes close slowly as if she's trying to get her thoughts straight before she peers at me once more.

"Your grandmother lives near the Iris River, you know? You should pay her a visit," she says oddly before releasing my hand and walking away, jarring her shoulder hard into Sev's on her way out.

I think through what she just said.

My grandmother.

I've never met my grandmother before . . .

A crawling sensation skitters along the flesh of my arms as if my body senses the bad that is about to come tumbling down into what little good I have left in my life.

I swallow that feeling back, but the turning feeling still lingers in the pit of my stomach.

It'll stay there. It'll stay until I've done exactly what Isabella's told me to do.

Whatever the hell that might be.

***

Warm fingers—almost hot—glide along my cheek, and my heavy lashes flutter at the gentle touch. A thumb skims my lower lip, pulling a sigh from my lungs as that hand trails lower along my throat.

My eyes slowly open to the purest look of love I've ever seen.

I just never expected it from Ryke.

I catch his big hand in mine as I take in the bruising covering the gashes along his throat.

"You should be resting," I say on barely a whisper, snuggling into his side as we lie on my bed, holding each other a bit more intimately than we probably should.

"And you should be awake instead of napping. That makes us even, Crow." His smile calms my heart.

He's right. I should be awake. I must have dozed off as the four of us were waiting for the dawn. It beams in brightly now across my wooden floors. It shines down on the two other men sleeping soundly in my room.

Zaviar sits in the chair in the corner, and his head's tipped so far back, I can't see his eyes, but the steady rise and fall of his smooth chest tells me he's fast asleep.

Krave lies flat on his back with his arm tucked under me as though he held me through the night.

I hope he did.

To my surprise, Damien's sideways on the mattress, his legs still dangling off the edge as if he's prepared to stand and leave at any moment. His golden locks fan across Krave's stomach where he rests his head along the hard lines of the incubus's body.

And Krave's other hand, it's gently resting against Damien's shoulder. His *bare* shoulder . . . that unfiltered sex magic is just lying there against Damien's skin.

The morning erection outlined beneath Damien's jeans tells me that magic is in full *raging* effect.

"Pen checked in on me." Ryke tells me on a hushed tone. I lock eyes with him and there's a deep heat there in his shadowed green gaze. "She asked me what she could do to make me feel better."

Oh no. Did … did something happen between them? Something sexy? Something my mind doesn't have the nerve to imagine for the sake of my heart?

"I told her *you*." A small smile pulls at his lips and I don't understand at first. "I told her you made me feel better." My heart stutters. "She said she hates the idea of keeping me in the demon quarters. She said I could stay with you as long as I wanted. As much as I wanted."

A stinging sensation trails down my collarbone. It hesitates there for a single long second before drifting down the V-neck of my T-shirt. My stunned gaze lingers on him and his deep emerald eyes hold mine as his fingers ever so slowly slide down along my breast, teasing the flesh of my skin with his light touch. He watches me watching him as we both listen to the pounding of my slamming heart.

I want him to touch me. I want him to distract me. I want—

His fingers skim over my nipple with so much tingling pain, I gasp in response to the minimal touch. A rough beard scrapes my jaw as his mouth presses to the curve of my neck. He kisses there with a flick of his tongue in a rush of heat that spirals right down to my center. A gasp like a cry of pleasured pain cuts from my lips.

"You have to be quiet, baby," he whispers against my

ear. "I don't think it'd be good for us if you were caught with three demons in your bed." He says all that while pushing my shirt up and taking my nipple fully into his mouth, sucking so hard, my head falls back without remembering a single word of the warning he just gave.

His big hands send fire through my veins as he pushes a path up my ribs, and then shoves my shirt up higher for himself. He flicks his tongue out across my sensitive flesh once more before taking in the sight of my body beneath him.

A growl of delicious approval hums from his throat.

And then he's crawling lower down my body.

My eyes open slowly and I almost say something—anything—but he jerks my jeans roughly down before a single sound comes out. He pulls my jeans and panties off entirely. Big hands wrap around my inner thighs, and he spreads me wide for himself as he lowers down between my legs. Warm breath licks at my flesh. Even warmer fingers draw slow lazy lines across my hips, my pubic bone, my lips . . . but he never dips lower. He rubs his tingling touch back and forth between my legs until I feel it deep within my sex. I'm trembling beneath his big hand, and it builds to a pulse within my chest.

"Please, Ryke. Please," I beg.

"Please what?" he asks on a gravelly voice like sex and sin.

My lashes flutter, and I swallow hard to think about what he wants, and what I want, and how they're both the same fucking thing.

"Please touch me, and suck me, and fuck me so hard that everyone knows your name from how loud I'm screaming it." I almost smile—almost.

But then his growling response is humming across my clit as his mouth opens wide and takes as much of my pussy into it as he can. The width of his tongue covers my sex, sliding deep inside before lapping me up and swirling hard across my clit. My fingers push through his short hair, and that's the only thing grounding me, it feels like. His tongue fucks me hard, lashing against my sex, diving deep and thrusting hungrily with so much intensity, I shiver beneath him as an ache tightens low in my core.

His big hands hold me in place against his mouth, and the thrumming feeling inside of me grows with every shaking breath I gasp for.

He stops.

The movement of the earth stops right along with him.

My eyes open slowly. His heated gaze holds mine. And then he sucks hard and demandingly against my clit, his teeth raking just slightly as he draws out all the pent-up sounds inside me. Lustful pleading moans fill the room, and still he works my clit in pulsing sensations.

Two big fingers slide down my wetness. He slides back and forth there for a moment.

And then he thrusts deep inside. His thick digits thrust, arching up at the perfect angle as he takes the flat of his tongue and rolls it across the sensitive and throbbing nub that holds all of his attention. He does it all again and again and again.

Until pain and pleasure collide together like white hot embers within me. It clashes and rolls within my core in a freefalling feeling of total ecstasy.

And then I'm screaming his name on a trembling, gasping tone.

I'm pulling at his hair and trying to bring him closer to me. I need him closer.

I need him inside me.

Now.

But when I lean up on my shaking elbows, Zaviar's staring down at us. So is Krave. And so is Damien.

All three of them now have an interesting outline pressing against their jeans. Krave's eyes hold a sparking interest. He's waiting. Either to join or to watch or both, I'm not sure.

Damien's breathing heavy, and he isn't as manic about it as Krave, but I can tell he wants the same thing.

But there's one major angelic cockblock in the room.

"Aren't you supposed to be visiting your grandmother, Crow?" Zaviar asks calmly with a condescending arch of his brow.

"Aren't you supposed to be able to keep your dick soft around women who aren't angels?" I cut back at him with lashing words, even if they are still breathless and weak-sounding.

A slow smirk, cruel and carving, pulls across his hard features. "Don't flatter yourself. Wet fae pussy isn't anything special. One of the reasons your kind is considered beneath us is because you'll cum for anyone. Fucking is just fucking for fae. Seraphs are known for their endurance, little Crow. We choose our own because our own have the power to please us. Unlike the weaker races." He folds his big arms across his chest, the muscles along his sides flexing those swooping words across his ribs.

Without Regret. Without Remorse.

My chin lifts to his harsh words. "Well, Remorseless, don't let all those godly friends of yours know I made you cum without ever touching your endurance-blessed dick." His features fall just slightly, and I don't know why I have to twist the knife even more. "Maybe also don't tell them your demonic brother made me cum better than you ever did."

Without Regret. Without Remorse.

I don't believe that for a single fucking second.

If I did, he wouldn't be staring at me with so much pain in his deep blue eyes right now. And I wouldn't feel sick to my stomach for putting that pain there.

CHAPTER TWELVE
To Grandmother's House We Go
Aries

The enormous leaves hang above like an umbrella, blocking out the warm sunlight as we trail quietly toward the trickling sound of the Iris River. There's a path here, worn and broken in by many hikes from our busy kingdom to the quiet countryside.

Many have taken this dirty road. But I haven't.

"I've never met my grandmother," I say, not sure who I'm speaking to but needing to say it all the same.

Damien glances my way, but his attention slips to someone else when they, too, confess something astonishing.

"I have," Krave whispers, looking at me from the corner of his depthless eyes.

My boots scuff the dirt from how abruptly I stop.

"You've met my grandmother?" I cock my head at the mysterious incubus and all the secrets he keeps.

Krave's lips open and then close slowly before he tries once more. "Your father visits her every year on his birthday."

It's a secret. He just gave me a secret of his previous handler . . .

"He forbids his children and his family, everyone, he forbids them to see her. But every year on his birthday, he'd come to spend an hour with her." Krave's so serious right now, it just puts me even more on edge.

On his fucking birthday. Not hers. How fucking selfish can my father be?

"Why?" I ask like a command.

The incubus just shakes his head. "I don't know. He'd never say. I'd accompany him to her cottage, but I was never allowed inside." He swallows before he seems to remember something. "I met her once. She followed him out into the night air, and she looked at me like she'd seen a ghost. She said she missed me, but we couldn't meet like this anymore."

I blink at him, unsure what to do with that information. He shrugs, and I press for more. "Was—was she happy? Cruel? Hurt?" Why would he have kept us away from her?

Why?

Long, glittering black fingers slip over mine, and with a tingling touch, he holds my hand in his. "She—she was confused, Ari. She asked where her crown was. She said she wanted to go home." His lips stay parted, but no other words come out for several beats of my heart. And then, unfortunately, he says more. "She has memory fleet, love. Her memories have dissolved, and it's left her with a helpless sense of loss."

The pounding of my heart is pressing so hard, it's like I can feel it the moment it breaks.

"Oh," I whisper.

The four of us stand there as I stare at the dirt between us. I study the divots and the twigs. I consider each little particle of nothingness as this sense of hurt settles in my chest.

I've never met her. But even if I did, she wouldn't remember me anyway.

She doesn't even remember her own life.

And Isabella sent me to her.

Why?

To help her?

How?

"Do you still want to go?" Damien asks gently.

I nod before he even gets the question fully out. "Yes. Yes, we should go. She'll probably like the company." The fucking company she should have had all her life. Instead of being shut away far from the castle like a sickness being contained.

The rest of the short trip I spend digging my boots into the dirt with every hard stomp I take toward the beautiful shimmering river. Light reflects off of it in shining white colors. It's calming. It's peaceful.

At least she has this piece of perfection to keep her company. It's a nice little relaxing slice of nature.

It would be good for the elder fae to grow old with.

It'd be nice for a senior to rest near.

It—a blade strikes out and slices just beneath my jaw. "You newcomers dropping by to steal my crown?" A woman barks out at us. The sharp end of her blade never wavers for a single second. Which is impressive when I spot the small old woman holding the hilt of it.

Her big black wings are graying at the ends. They match the silver color of her long waving hair.

Grandmother Hyval.

"Your Highness," Krave says with a sweeping bow. "Your son, Lord Gravier, sent us for an exclusive meeting regarding the renovation of your castle that you're still waiting on." His charm oozes out in layers that make me gag.

Her gray eyes get a long-lost look in them as she stares at the incubus. "Gravier sent you?" she asks absently, as though she hasn't heard his name possibly ever. As if she's only heard it in the echoes of her thoughts. "Gravier," she says once more, her features smoothing with a bit of remembrance slipping across the lines of her face. "Yes. I apologize. He should have sent word of your arrival beforehand."

"Yes, yes, he should have," Krave says with a quick nod.

Her frail hand sweeps back to the small wooden cottage seated near the riverside. "Please come in." Her thin ivory gown drags the dirt as her bare feet pad over to the little house.

We follow quietly behind her.

The boards let out a slow whine when my boots settle just inside the small home. I expected one of two things inside this house: immense luxury or immense poverty.

110

I didn't expect . . .

"Stones," Damien whispers.

Starting high above the window over the kitchen counter, there's a pile of stones tossed atop one another. The smooth black exterior of the little rocks looks polished. So flawless, they seem wet with a shine I can't take my eyes off of.

The black metal mantle holding up the thousands of little stones bows in the middle where more and more and more of the things continue to make trailing line around the entirety of the room. The mantle drifts down, uneven on some walls but still doing its job of containing all the shining rocks. The beam of metal juts out from the corner on the south wall and expands into a larger section that's big enough to host a breakfast at the castle. Instead of food on the table, it supports the thousands of stones that rest at the center of the room like an odd wishing well. If I toss a new stone onto that pile, will my heart's desire be granted?

Would I finally find peace in my life?

"They're remembrance stones," Hyval says, cutting through my thoughts and catching my attention when I spot her graying wings expand from her small frame. They carry her just a few gentle beats, and her dirty bare feet land on the smooth countertop. I'm surprised how steady her hands are as she lifts a large bowl above her head and pours out its contents onto the trail of piled stones. The trickling sound of water rushes from where she stands, it slides over all the rocks, rushing through the mantle's path that surrounds us. I listen to the sweet sound of gushing water.

Then it comes to a slow stop at the center of the room just inches away from me, where the largest of the mounds of stones are. In the middle there, with the rocks poised right into a towering heap of décor, it's like art.

Art I don't understand the meaning of one bit.

"Pick up that one nearest you," Hyval instructs as she floats down to the wooden floor after thoroughly watering her rocks.

The rock at the corner of the wooden stand is slick against my palm. It's light. It's the kind of thing you'd want to toss across a serene lake and count how many skips it beats across the water before sinking down into the deep nothingness.

I wait with it held in the palm of my hand, but . . . it's just a rock.

"It's a very nice rock, Hyval," I say with a small forced smile.

"*Queen* Hyval," she corrects.

"Yes, *Queen* Hyval," I say respectfully to my grandmother. The one who doesn't even know who I am.

"And you're using it wrong." Her gray hair swishes as she tilts her head at me, really staring at my features for a long moment. "You remind me of someone," she says with that shake of uncertainty she had in her tone when we first arrived.

Do I tell her the young son she had grew up? He grew up hateful, and he tried to instill that hate into the three children he had.

"I've never had the pleasure of meeting you, my Queen," I say instead, the smile on my lips nearly falling into a wavering frown.

Her silver eyes light up a little with a soft smile that blooms pain through my chest.

I look like her. I remind her of herself, but she doesn't remember herself.

She . . .

Fuck!

Why! Why did my father keep her out here alone, with only the crumbling memories in her mind to keep her company?

I bite my lower lip hard enough to almost compare with the pain that's building in my chest, and I have to turn away from her kind eyes to face the wall and feign interest in the rocks that look just like all the others. Except these ones are so glistening, they reflect the dampness in my eyes as I peer down on them.

Gentle fingers slide down my spine over my shirt, but Damien never says a word.

I push my hands over my face slowly before tangling them through my hair. A deep breath hits my lungs, and I blink away the lingering pain until I'm sure I can look at her without bursting into tears.

I smooth my hands on my jeans and turn back around.

Except she's gone.

"Where did she go?" I hiss to the four men standing there, like they let her escape.

"Calm down," Krave says with a tilt of his head toward the open door. "She's out watering the river."

"Watering the river?" Zaviar repeats with a lift of his dark brows.

Krave nods as if it's all in a normal day's work.

I stand there looking out the wooden doorframe, watching the gray-haired woman sway to a humming tune as

113

she dips her bowl into the river, and then slowly trickles that water right back down into the sloshing running water.

She's . . . happy, I think. Obliviously happy. Tormented with happiness.

My heart hurts looking at her. My fingers run absent-mindedly over the smooth surface of the warm rock in my hand. I worry at it, sliding across the rounded edges over and over and over again.

Until my surroundings disappear.

Fluttering lashes blink repeatedly. They fan in front of me as I gaze out the glass window at the rain pounding down on the river water gushing ferociously. White lightning strikes hard with a howling gust of wind alongside the little home.

My sight isn't my own. My body moves at the pace of someone else's steps, and the movement and the flow of my gait is wobbling. Entirely not my own.

What the fuck?

I peer out the side window near the little door, and I realize I'm still in Hyval's cottage. But it's no longer morning. Nightfall casts across the dark sky, and I'm alone in the tiny house.

Her face peers back at me in the reflection of the window. Her face . . . and mine.

I want to gasp, but once again, I'm reminded this isn't my body.

Total serene calmness is all Hyval has within her gentle-beating heart.

"Dravle simply cannot stay here. It's romantic but . . . it's drafty. Bitterly cold. I—" She turns us to look around. Her attention shifts from the kitchen counter to the stack of stones in the center of the room. She's alone. "*I want to go home*," she whispers to only herself.

Her dry lips close, and I feel the confusion in her mind. I feel her fear prickle across her flesh. She just won't show it. Her shaking breath slips from her lips, and she starts quietly toward the bed in the next room. At the last second, she sets the stone down next to the others.

And then the bright morning sunlight flashes before my eyes.

"Aries, are you fuckin' okay? Aries?" Strong hands grip my shoulders, and the anxiety rushing through his words shake through me as his hold on me wavers with a little jolt.

I look up at intense blue eyes. Those dark eyebrows of his are shaded over his eyes, just as they always are, but not from anger this time.

Zaviar's worried. About me.

"I'm fine." I blink slowly, my hand loose against the stone as I try to understand what just happened. "The remembrance stones capture moments. She's capturing moments for herself. She knows she's forgetting, and she's trying to help herself," I tell them, looking around the room and finding more and more of the black stones shining in hiding spots all around the house. One rests atop the door frame. Another is dropped in the corner. Several line the floors along the wall, and I spot even more glinting in her bedroom. They're everywhere. Thousands of them.

And one of them has what Isabella sent me here for.

"One of these stones has captured something important. We need to go through the stones one by one and find what Isabella knows is hidden here."

"Are you fucking kidding? That'll take months, Crow," Zaviar's calloused hands slide down my arms, and he winces, turning his head from me and pushing his fingers over the bridge of his nose.

I tilt my head at him, but he ignores me.

"Why can't you just ask the little shadow cunt what she knows?" Zaviar demands, shaking off whatever he felt earlier as he glares at me with that lovely little aggravation that I'd almost missed.

"Because the guard doesn't trust Aries," Krave says for me.

My attention cuts to the overly watchful incubus.

But he's right.

And though it takes many more grumbles and a lot more cursing from Zaviar, we get to work. Hours pass in a haze of someone else's mind. I watch Hyval from the beginning. I watch her as she starts to realize in the political meetings in the offices of the castle that she's forgetting things here and there. She starts the stones early in her life to remind her of agendas and important key figures in her life. At one point, she cries.

She's young and beautiful. Alone after the death of her husband. But entirely alone to the life she leads. And she's forgetting it, bit by bit.

They whisper around her. Her ladies in waiting and her advisors. They whisper when she exits rooms.

"Headless Hyval called out for her husband again in the middle of the night. The poor King died five years ago. Let him rest."

"I heard old Headless Hyval shook hands with her son this morning and asked if he was the new war

commander."

"Did you hear Headless Hyval blew a trade deal with the Kingdom of Crowns in the north? Couldn't remember the bloody King's name even though she's met him a hundred times. She was at his son's wedding, for fae fuck's sake."

"Do you think . . . do you think we should consider carefully suggesting resignation for Headless Hyval?"

It's late in the night when my eyes flash open. The pounding of my heart is so overwhelming, it's all I hear.

It's all I hear until bickering cuts in.

"Stop watching it! It's rude!" Damien yells across the room as he tosses another black stone in his messy pile in front of him.

Krave shakes his head at the man. He's seated cross-legged on the floor and has just one stone in front of him.

One.

"It's not rude," Krave argues with a half-smile and a wave of his hand. "It's research."

"What are you talking about?" I finally ask, like I haven't solved our problem only to be tossed right back in the Broadway shit show of The Demonic Housewives TV special.

Gods, no wonder people fear going to hell.

These two would be there to bicker their brains out.

"I've gone through a hundred and two stones, and Krave keeps coming back to the one where your dear old grams fucks an incubus named Dravle." Ryke pushes his big hands down his face and releases a long slow breath.

"She didn't just fuck him. Don't be crude. They were in love," Krave says with a slightly dreamy, slightly lustful sigh.

My lips are parted as I look from one man to the next and still have no words to solve their petty argument.

"Anyway," I say instead. "I know what Isabella was trying to tell me."

"Thank fuck," Zaviar growls, his eyes closing tightly as he steels his jaw against what seems to be a migraine. His hand shoves over his left pectoral muscle, though.

Krave, Damien, and Ryke stand at once. When Zaviar stands, his knees give out. He lands on all fours with a shaking groan.

I'm in front of him in seconds. "What's wrong with you?"

"Nothing," he says on a harsh breath.

"Zaviar!" My hands push over his smooth shoulders, but his head hangs low as his pink wings shake from how hard he's breathing.

"I'm fine," he repeats, his tone still screaming the opposite.

His arms give out, and he lowers himself down on his knees and forearms, breathing through whatever pain he won't admit to.

"He shouldn't be here," Damien whispers.

"Shut the fuck up," Zaviar snaps.

My own breath cuts out as I blink down at the beautiful angel who's sitting in a worshiping position.

He doesn't belong here.

He certainly doesn't belong bound to me.

And yet, he refuses to leave.

"Come on. I'm getting you help," I say, hauling him to his feet. He stumbles, and Damien ends up slipping an arm around him to keep him upright.

But he does come.

Because he needs help. *Now.*

Even if we both know it'll come at a price.

CHAPTER THIRTEEN
A Vow
Zaviar

I was starting to think the castle was worse than the treehouse with Corva looming over us.

Gods, was I fuckin' wrong.

Corva is so much worse than the assholes prancing around the castle pretending they're better than everyone else because they're sinless.

Corva though, she's not petty.

She's deadly.

Her smoky black hair wafts around her pale face as she tilts her head this way and that from above me. I lie flat on the wooden couch and hold back every searing sting of pain that stabs through my heart. It feels like my heart is splitting. Like—like it wants to tear in half and just end my agony right here, right now.

"He needs to go back to the gods," Corva says to her sister, who stands only inches away from me.

Aries hasn't left my side all night. Her pretty face is pinched in a look of concern that I've never seen her have for me.

That look warms my cracking heart.

"He, uh . . . he can't go back," Aries whispers.

Everyone in the room shifts to face her.

"What the fuck do you mean, I can't go back?" My teeth grind together with slicing pain shooting once more through my chest.

Corva's thin brows lift in surprise as she looks at her little sister. The smile on her lips is unsettling, to say the least.

That smile clings to her lips as she speaks. "You bound him, didn't you?"

"Ahh," Krave says with a smirk as well.

The two of them are not fuckin' helping right now. "What!" I holler. "They did that demon binding. It's for demons. It's fucking useless on seraphs."

"Ha-ha, that's where you're wrong, my pretty pink-feathered friend," Krave says with a shake of his long glittering finger.

Fucking incubus.

I grimace once more, but this time, it has nothing to do with physical pain.

"It's a ritual created by high fae magic. You're bound to my sister," Corva says with gleaming excitement in her eyes.

"I—I have to go back," I say sternly.

"Yes. Yes. You do. But when a binding is stretched,"

Corva claps her hands together, and as she slowly pulls them away, a thread of golden magic disperses between her palms. It becomes thinner and thinner. Until it snaps with sparking colors. "It won't be pretty for you, Angel."

"Fuck," I growl out, my palm pressing over my pec to sooth the carving agony.

"If you stay, it'll hurt. And if you leave Aries, it'll really fucking hurt," Krave explains in layman's-blunt-stupid-fucking-incubus terms.

I'd say something back to him, but the next jolt of throbbing terror hits my heart like I'm dying with a full breath in my lungs. Dying while my head throws back.

And a beautiful gift from the gods looks down on me. "I'm so sorry, Zav." Her tone is hushed and intimate along my ear. Her breath skims my skin while her fingers thread through my hair.

Maybe I am dying.

I'm dying a sweet miserable death that I deserve.

"Can you help him? Can you reverse the bindings?" Aries cries, her voice shaking so hard, it hurts to hear.

"No." Corva's long smoky dress fumes around her as she turns away from us. "You can pass the binding along to someone else, allowing them to inherit your angel. That's the best you have right now," she calls over her shoulder as though she's done for the night.

She's so much fucking worse than the pretentious castle fucks.

"That's bullshit! Numb his pain! I know you can." Aries is standing and storming across the floors to her sister so fast, it sets the entire room on edge. The men around me shift their stance toward the woman dressed in all black.

If Corva were to so much as scratch Aries, those three idiots would die avenging her slight discomfort.

Corva's eyes are so bright, they're like hellfire glinting in the dim lighting. Her amusement is enough to give me chills. "I'll help him," Corva says with that slow crawling smile catching her lips. "But I want something in exchange."

Ryke groans at the sound of that statement.

I glance toward him and his thick etching scars are all I can focus on while the two women talk less than three feet from me. I can't help but compare Aries's smooth flawless body to Ryke's in this moment.

He's been touched by Corva's dark fae magic for over a century. But it all started with him needing one thing from her.

Just like Aries does right now.

"Aries. Aries, don't." My hand pushes beneath me, but when I try to sit up, my arm gives out, and my head bangs against the wooden armrest. "Fucckk," I hiss.

"What do you want?" Aries continues on as if I never said a godsamn thing.

Corva's smile dips. It falters into a low frown. "I want to be with my family, Ari." Her tone is so gentle, it's alarming. I've known this woman for a while now, and I've never fucking heard that kind of sincerity.

I don't believe it for a fuckin' second.

Aries's iron-like eyes shift across Corva's face as seconds pass in silence. "I know," she finally says.

Fuck me.

"Aries," I call to her, but once more, I'm just the forgotten dying seraph in the background of everyone's thoughts. Pain slices through me, and I groan from it as much as I'm groaning in annoyance.

"I want to come back to court," Corva the Conniving Cunt says.

"I know." Aries looks at her sister with too much kindness in her pretty eyes.

"You'll help me, then? You'll help me come back to the castle?"

No. Fuck no. "Aries," I whisper on a shaking breath, my entire body trembling with agony.

Damien looks back at me. "Shh," he says with a small shake of his head, like I'm interrupting a fucking family moment here.

What the fuck is this shit? Why is no one listening to me? I have one little heart condition, and all of a sudden, I'm the horse looking down the barrel of a shotgun?

"I can't trust you, Corva." Aries lifts her chin high in that sexy little dominant stance of hers.

That's my fucking girl!

Gods, she's so much smarter than she looks. Sometimes. I mean, she's . . . whatever.

"You're one to throw stones," Corva says with an arch of her brow. "How's Nathiale, Aries? How's my sweet little brother? Tell me."

Aries doesn't flinch from those sharp-spoken words. She doesn't even blink with the confrontation thrown at her feet. She's fucking fearless.

Why am I so turned on right now?

"I can't trust you, and you can't trust me. Why in all the realms would you think anything has changed in the last twenty-three years, Corva? This is what father raised us to be. Not family, but not quite enemies, either. We can't trust each other. But we can help each other."

Shit. Aries might act like nothing gets to her. But her family, they get in nice and deep under her skin, it seems.

"Take a vow with me," Corva says swiftly. And all of a sudden, I'm pushing to my feet. I stumble just slightly, but I right myself on the corner of the couch.

"She's not fucking doing that," I growl out.

Finally—fucking finally—Aries looks at me. Her eyes are big and shining in a way I couldn't see before. It cuts into me deeper than the pain that's already tearing me open.

"You should rest," she whispers.

"I'm fine," I say for what must be the hundredth time.

"Aries Sinclaire, I vow never to harm you, never to hurt you, never to kill you," Corva announces in a scripture-type tone that chills my bones.

Aries turns to her sister then, her chin held high, her features fearless.

"Corva of the Unknown, I vow never to harm you, never to hurt you, never to kill you," Aries repeats.

Fuck.

The two women clasp hands and pull one another in nice and close. Their heads tilted down to their joined hands held between them.

"Until I take my last breath," Corva whispers, breathing purposefully across the back of their knuckles.

"Until I take my last breath," Aries agrees, doing the exact same, washing their hands with the unbreakable vow she's spoken.

Silver light mingles together with ashen smoke. It slips from their palms and hovers around them, encompassing them in the powerful vow they just promised one another.

She said she doesn't trust Corva, but on some level, she does.

Trust is a dangerous thing. Not enough can get you killed. And too much, well that can get you killed even faster.

Chapter Fourteen
Time for Healing
Aries

I stand at a close distance as my sister lowers herself down to where Zaviar lies on the wooden couch. He can say he's fine all he wants, but I can see the way he can hardly catch his breath.

The righteous bastard.

Damien shifts so he's peering out the window into the deep darkness of the night. Ryke tenses at my side, but he watches my sister begin her work without looking away. It surprises me how much Krave is paying attention. There's no elaborate smile on his face. He seems almost worried.

"Hold still," Corva instructs as she slides her index finger over Zaviar's chest and settles above his heart.

I swallow hard, and I don't know when it happened, but without realizing it, I'm holding Zaviar's warm hand in mine. His dark lashes flutter as he looks down on our joined hands. He peers up at me with a question burning in those sweet blue eyes of his.

Someone's hurt him too much in his life. That's where all that anger and aggression comes from inside of him.

I won't let anyone else hurt him. Not ever again.

At least . . . after my sister's done with him, that is.

Her finger presses hard into his skin, and the tips of her black nail drag across his flesh with a sizzling sound.

Muscles jump along his jaw as he steels his body hard, clenching every single muscle against the feel of Corva's rune magic.

She's part demon. And now, Zaviar has a little bit of that essence inside him, too.

I can't help but pause for a response from my own demon inside of me.

Catherine's silent.

I shake my head at the strange feeling of emptiness her quietness brings me.

"There," Corva says when she's made several slashing lines intertwine over Zaviar's heart. It's harsh and deep-cutting, but it heals quickly with fumes of black smoke. It turns to a thin scar immediately. "How do you feel?" Corva asks with a tilt of her long black hair.

"Fucking fantastic," Zaviar spits with a curl of his lips.

"Does it hurt?" My fingers lift, and I'm tracing the cutting lines across his skin as I speak.

The muscles jump beneath my touch. His throat clears hard as he shifts beneath my fingers.

"No. Not at all," he says on an odd rasp.

There's always this slicing look of hate kept on reserve in his gaze. As he looks up at me right now, that cruel sentiment isn't in his eyes at all. He looks . . . at ease. For once in his life.

Why do I like you so much, Remorseless?

It isn't good for my heart, I know that much. My past. Krave himself has taught me to not get attached to someone who can never be yours.

But look how that turned out . . .

"We should stay the night tonight. And possibly tomorrow," I announce.

Zaviar's lips curl back into their natural habitat of disgusted annoyance.

There's my angel.

"Ari, you said you'd figured it all out, though," Krave whispers, his hesitant gaze slipping from me to my sister.

Corva gives a false smile and continues to watch us with rapt attention.

Krave doesn't want to say too much in front of her. And neither do I.

"Let's just stay. For tonight. It's late, and we should rest anyway."

Ryke passes a skeptical look to Damien, but Damien's still watching his brother like his attention itself is keeping the angel safe.

No one responds to my new strange life choices.

I have four strong men surrounding me. Men who have taken magic straight to their heart. Men who have defied heaven and hell just to find their own path in these realms. Men who have changed my life forever.

And not one of these fuckers has the demon balls to question me.

I shove a long sigh from my lungs and finally grab Zaviar's hand. His dark eyebrows lift in surprise as I pull him to his feet. And continue to hold his warm comforting hand as I lead him past my still watchful sister. I grab Ryke's big hand at the last minute and create a sort of train, pulling along my silent men through the winding wooden house. Four sets of heavy boots pound in unison behind me as I guide them upstairs. It's a repetitive sound that storms through my head and slowly whisks away all the tumbling thoughts there with the thrilling idea that I'm leading them . . . to their bed.

Cold air sifts in, and it hits my face as I trail higher and higher. The steps give way, and then nothing but netting sways before me in the deep darkness of the night.

The moonlight scatters in through the enormous leaves above. It hints at the thin lines that cross all along the nest that these men used to love so much.

"I always thought this bouncy bed was just a kinky setup for you guys to lure women in here," Krave says huskily, breaking the silence.

Ryke's deep laughter follows, but none of us really say anything in response.

Until Damien speaks.

"No woman had ever slept here. Just Aries," he says on a breath that's just a bit too breathless.

A shiver slides over my skin, suddenly making me all too aware of how loud my heart's beating.

Why did that sound so romantic? It's just a bed,

Aries.

And then I'm thinking of Catherine. She'd tell me if I was being ridiculous or not. She'd snap me out of my emotions faster than anyone.

But my advisor I always ridiculed in the past . . . isn't there.

Why's she silent? Why isn't she there anymore? What did I do? Did I lose her?

I pushed too far. I slipped into the past of someone else's life. I was in Hyval's life the way Catherine was always in mine.

And I fucked something up by pushing too far.

I always fuck it up in the end.

Warm breath hits my ear as rough palms graze along my arms in a calming back-and-forth sweep, "What's wrong, Aries?" Damien rasps, the heat of his words dancing across my flesh.

His smooth skin beneath my palms covers the chiseled lines of his muscles as I push my way up his chest and lean into his perfect body. My lips are just beneath his when he dips his head down low. His warmth surrounds me. He'll protect me for the rest of our lives.

But he'll never protect me from me.

I shove aside that thought fast and hard as I press my lips to his.

He doesn't respond immediately. Soft lips tense beneath mine. Until my tongue flicks against his mouth, and he opens to me without hesitation. Hands clamp hard over my hips as he brings me against him like he's fighting for control in this nirvana of lust between us.

He holds me close, and I let him, but my wings

spread out wide behind me, and I pull him away. I bring him right where I want him without asking and without waiting.

My frame jars against his as his back hits the netting with a slight bounce. My legs part, and I'm straddled above him, just the way he likes.

Just the way I like.

"Gods, Aries," he murmurs against my lips between hot kisses and sharp bites of my teeth. "Just talk to me," he pleads.

But he never stops that delicious feel of his tongue sliding against mine.

"Later," I promise.

I'll talk later. I'll worry later. I'll hurt later.

For now, I just want to feel good.

With a groan, he seems to give in. And fuck, does he give in good.

His hips rock against mine, the friction of our clothes is as rewarding as it is frustrating.

"Take your pants off," I command on a breathless tone.

His hands shove between us like he's bound to the sound of my voice alone. He fumbles as I lift my hips for him, but he can't work the button, it seems.

Long steady fingers slide up and then down my stomach from beneath my shirt. A tremble follows his alluring touch, and I know immediately who it is.

"Let me help," Krave says with a soft addicting tone.

Damien groans a growling sound against my lips, and it makes my sex clench at the feel of it.

Krave's palm pushes against my center, cupping me from over my jeans hard and rough before doing what he offered to begin with.

When his magical fingers make contact with Damien's sensitive flesh, I know it immediately. Damien jerks beneath me, leaning up to devour the taste of my desire. His normally sweet kisses become demanding, dominating.

"Fuck," he growls, his hips rocking hard against something I can't see, but I want so, so badly to feel.

"I could watch the good in you fight the bad all fucking day, Fallen." Krave's wrist rolls against my lower stomach, and it causes Damien to bite my lip, his sharp teeth trailing even lower as he snips at my jaw line, kissing and hurting and soothing my flesh as he works his way down my throat. "Show Aries a little taste of that bad, Damien. Show her how good it feels."

My head tilts back for the consuming sensation of his mouth, hot and heavy against my skin. Just as my lashes flutter shut, he flips me.

The breath knocks from my lungs as I bounce against the netting.

"Take your shirt off," Damien commands on a voice I've never heard from him before.

His cock juts up toward his navel, and the length of it curves just slightly to the left. I study the powerful sight of him.

He looks like a fallen god instead of an angel. Big black wings loom behind his golden appearance. Messy hair falls in his dark chestnut eyes, no longer looking sweet as honey but darker. Deadlier.

My fingers spread over my stomach, just above my hips, and I hold his gaze as I slide my palms over my ribs, across the curve of my breasts, ever so slowly over my nipples, and then finally over my head.

"Fuck," someone else says from behind the two men looking down on me.

My attention flicks to the two shadows. I can't see Zaviar and Ryke, but I feel them watching.

Ryke shifts on his feet, and I want him here. I want him with me. I want him in me.

"Ryke," I whisper without air in my lungs.

"Don't fucking look at him," Damien says with eerie calmness. "Look at me."

I blink, and I can't help but think about his brother in this moment. Sometimes, sometimes the violence of his brother slips out of Damien's mouth, and it's so surprising, it's hard to take it all in.

"Take off your jeans." He's still kneeling over me, but he leans back, his hands patiently on his knees as he waits for me to do as I'm told.

Krave's eyes flash, and I feel him eating up every move I make.

My fingers trail down the valley between my breasts, and it feels good to make them want me without ever touching them. It's erotic in a way I've never felt before. With the heat of their attention, it's like someone else is touching me. Delicate fingers ghost over the soft skin between my hips. They unsnap my jeans and slide with feather-light pressure across my thighs. They come up slow and teasingly between my legs, brushing over my center before coming right back down and pushing the clothes away entirely. I shimmy out of them and continue to stroke my fingers back and forth along the wetness of my black panties.

Damien's lips part with heavy breaths as he focuses on those two fingers.

My hips lift to meet the gentle touch of my fingertips.

"Want more?" I ask quietly, the cool wind teasing my flesh and my nipples as I lie spread out for them all to see.

I glance to Krave. He's unbuttoning his own jeans as he watches the stroking movement of my hand between my thighs.

"Yes," Damien rasps out, glancing to Krave for only a moment as he speaks. His warm eyes meet mine, and he makes my legs shift when his big hand wraps around his own shaft.

My body feels like sex and power. It's sensual magic that makes me forget everything aside from the men surrounding me.

My palm lifts higher, my fingers slip just under the band of my panties.

But I stop.

"Make Krave feel good, and I'll make me feel good," I tell him instead.

Damien's hand wrapped around himself stops moving. He looks to the incubus at his side. Krave's brows lift like he's as surprised by what I just said as I am.

It's a flip of dominance. Damien likes me taking care of him. I know he does. Our relationship is taking care of one another. He's strong, but . . .

Will he take my command as I did his?

His hand lifts toward Krave. I watch with heavy attention. I wait with pent-up patience for him to wrap his big hand ever so slowly around Krave's length.

But he never does.

Instead, his palms settle gently on either side of Krave's sharp jaw. He leans in close, holding the incubus's curious gaze. Then Damien's lips brush sweetly against his. Krave's lashes flutter at how delicate the touch is.

Has anyone ever touched him like that?

It's a fleeting kiss, just a taste. And then Damien's mouth is trailing lower. I forget how much of a giver he is. And fuck, is he giving. His lips are light at the lowest part of the incubus's throat, but the scrape of his teeth isn't. He bites so hard, Krave groans, his hand lifting to clutch Damien, but he holds himself back. He doesn't dare make distracting magical contact with the man currently pleasing him. Lower and lower, Damien's mouth drawls a sinful path down the muscles of Krave's hard body. His big hands clamp over lean, carved hips. The flat of his tongue slides over the lines veering down, and Krave trembles hard from the teasing, flicking kiss.

But it seems Damien's just getting started. His mouth veers low with open-mouthed kisses just beneath Krave's hip. He bites and sucks and dips lower, but then comes right back up, never once touching Krave where he clearly wants and needs him.

"Damien," Krave rasps out, his hands fisting at his sides to stop himself from touching.

He's always so fucking careful with his hands. Meticulously careful.

That's how I know what he does next is entirely intentional.

"Damien," he whispers once more on the sweetest tone just before skimming his finger ever so lightly along the length of Damien's neck.

Damien's back arches, his arms shaking from the minor touch alone.

"Damien, love." Another sweeping touch right back up his neck before sliding even farther down. "Wrap your sinful mouth around my cock, and I promise I'll make you feel good," he whispers.

Another hard tremble shivers through the demon currently settled on his hands and knees. His head tips up. Their eyes clash in heated stares.

And then Damien's mouth lowers down. He presses a gentle kiss to the tip of Krave's dick. His tongue slides out oh-so-slowly to swirl lightly at the head of the smooth hard flesh. His lips part, and my breath catches as he slides his mouth down farther and farther over every prominent vein of Krave's hardness.

My legs shift together to ease the throbbing sensation that I'm doing absolutely nothing with.

"Didn't you promise to do something with those idle hands, Ari?" Krave asks on a shaking breath, his head tipping back to expose how much Damien's affecting him. He looks down on me through thick dark lashes. "Take that hand and slide your panties to the side, love," he whispers, licking his lips slowly as he watches me.

A shiver runs down my spine, and my back arches in response.

And I do as I'm told.

Fingers skim like a breath against my thigh. The thin panties hook around my index finger, and then cool air sweeps over the most sensitive part of me as I'm bared to the three men still watching intently.

"Spread those long legs. Show Ryke how wet you are for him. Show that angel what he'll never taste," Krave says on a cruel, cutting tone.

My legs shake as my thighs part wide and invitingly.

Groans kiss the wind from the shadows before me. I feel that sound rumble through my core, and I suddenly want someone against me more than I want the air in my lungs.

I want Ryke's big body between my thighs. I want Krave's dirty mouth against my pussy. I want Damien's hands all over my trembling body.

And I want—I fucking want every part of Zaviar.

Even if I know I'll never truly have him.

Krave gasps with a string of curses slipping out as he shoves his hands through Damien's hair and thrusts his hips hard and fast.

They're consumed with one another. And I'm still on display for men who are too, too far away.

"You going to fuckin' make yourself cum, Pretty Crow?" A steadier voice asks, and I can hear his smirk.

I want him nearer.

"Why don't you make me?"

It's a petty response, but I mean it so fucking much.

Make me cum, Zaviar. Fuck me. Feel so good until you forget the loyalty you have to your own kind. Fuck me. Use me. Own me.

But never, never leave me.

"You know I can't, Pretty Crow." His words are hesitant. Wanting. "If I did, though, how would you want me to do it?"

Ryke's low growling groan shudders out and just causes my breath to shudder even more.

These men are going to be the sexy death of me.

My fingers twitch as I think through what he just said to me.

"I'd want you to go slow so I could feel every part of you first." My index finger slides down my wet folds. The steady touch rubs back and forth against my slickness, almost grazing my clit but not quite.

Another cutting breath kisses the darkness, and I know Ryke's working himself now just like I am. Just like I want them to.

I close my eyes and imagine Zaviar's strong body caging me in from above. I remember the way his hands felt consuming and controlling against my skin.

My fingers push hard over my mound, and a gasp tears from my throat as my head falls back in a blissful memory.

"I'd want you to fuck me with your mouth. Worship me with that cruel mouth of yours. Lap up the taste of my cum and feel me fall apart in your arms before making me do it all over again with your cock buried deep inside me."

"Fucckk, Aries," Zaviar groans, and it's enough to make my core ache without him.

Fingers thrust in deep, forcing a moan from my lips as I try to imagine how good he'd make me feel. I try to imagine how hard he'd fuck me. I try to imagine how much he'd fill me so entirely, I'd be gasping against his lips for more and more and more.

But it isn't enough.

It's torment.

It's the worst pain to know you can have something.

But to also know it'll never be yours.

"Zaviar, come here," I fling my eyes open and listen to the silence. Only uneven breaths reply.

Is he scared? Is he terrified he'll fuck up his life just by being near me?

Wind swooshes down on me with the gentle sound of wings soaring above.

Mere seconds pass.

From behind, his hands slide beneath my shoulders, and he lifts me up into a sitting position. His warm chest meets my back, and I settle there in his arms as he hugs me from behind.

"I want you so fucking bad it hurts, Aries," he says in a tortured tone. His head drops to my shoulder, and I feel his pain seep into me. We're the same. He and I are so fucking alike, we're miserable together.

Miserably in love.

And I never even realized it.

Tears sting my eyes.

Warm hands slide up the underside of my thighs. A body cradles me as he settles in nice and close, bringing my legs up until my thighs are wrapped around his hips.

I'm wrapped around Ryke, and Zav is wrapped around me.

"Don't cry, Crow." Ryke tells me with a tilt of his head. "You're strong. You're too fucking strong to cry over something you'll always own. And you'll always own the four of us, baby. Don't you ever fucking forget that."

"Mmm," Krave says on an uneven sound of agreement.

I nod, but I can't stop the wetness from filling my eyes.

Not until Ryke's big body shifts closer. And closer.

Smooth skin brushes against my wetness. He teases the flesh between my thighs with languid thrusts that grind against my folds but never fill me.

His big hands are warm as he skims up my stomach and across my hips. With a hard jerk, he brings me closer. He holds me firmly against him. I'm shared between the two men in a way that allows me to feel both of their pounding heartbeats and all of their hungry heated breaths.

I peer over just long enough to see Krave hovering over Damien, their lips parted as Krave slides his tongue slowly over Damien's, kissing him so deeply I know he feels more than just faint friendship for the man beneath him.

They're connected. The bond they share with me only ties their feelings together even deeper.

But I know there's more than that. So much more.

Fingers tilt my chin up to the man staring down on me. Ryke's shining eyes drift to my lips, and his beard scrapes my skin as his mouth presses gently against mine. He takes my breath away as he ever so slowly slides in. His thickness makes me gasp against his parted lips.

"You said slow at first, right, baby?" His body is tense and hard as he takes his time to slide out so fucking slowly, I feel every single inch he has to offer.

He takes my breath away when he sinks in, taking his time filling me entirely as he holds himself above me. Over and over and over again, he thrusts in with languid strokes, stealing my gasps and harboring my cries of empty breaths.

"You're so fuckin' sexy, Aries," Zaviar whisper against my throat, his hand snaking across my chest to hold my chin up high for him as he presses his mouth against my neck. His filthy words and heated breath consume me while Ryke's body works me with meticulous pounding thrusts.

"Ryke, please," I beg, my hands pushing across the deep lines scarring his chest.

"Please, what, baby?" he asks as he presses a sweet taunting kiss to my lips.

My fingers slip around the back of his neck, and I jerk him against my mouth. I only pull back long enough to sink my teeth into his lower lip, and as he groans a sound of pain and pleasure, I tell him, "Fuck me harder, Ryke."

Big hands slide down all the way to my ass, and he lifts me up just slightly, positioning me just how he likes before driving down hard with so much force, it knocks the breath from my lungs. My head throws back against Zaviar, and the two men hold me between them as I fall apart. A slamming slapping sound accompanies my jagged moans of lustful desire.

Zaviar kisses my neck, his hand roaming low to slide between our damp bodies. His fingers slide over my sex, and he pinches my clit before rubbing it harder and harder. Ryke and Zaviar give me unfiltered ecstasy, and I release it all on screams that kiss the silence. The stars above me shine in my eyes even as I close my lids and let the throbbing tension within me explode into shattered pieces that tingle through every inch of my body.

Ryke thrusts harder and harder and more and more recklessly until he slams in once more.

And then stops with a shuddering breath kissing my skin.

He looks down on me with the sweetest look in his hooded eyes. I feel every part of him against me. I feel his heart, and I know he feels mine.

I want to love him. I just don't want to mess up his life more than I already have.

I don't want him to be like the others.

And so, I'll never say the words that are caught in my throat right now.

I blink the streaming colors from my eyes, and all I can hear is the knocking of my pounding heart. It drowns out the whisper along my ear.

But I know what Zaviar just said.

I know by the quietness of his tone. I know by the gentleness of his hands. I know by the way he kisses my ear after he says it.

"I love you so fuckin' much, Aries."

I stare up at the heavens above. I glare into the beautiful starlight.

And I curse the gods for giving me a man I can never keep.

CHAPTER FIFTEEN
Patience
Ryke

She looks like an angel when she sleeps.

A beautiful dark angel. Surrounded by so much hell, it'll eat her alive.

"Why do you think she wants to stay?" Damien asks, breaking the quiet as he pulls her closer against his chest.

He's still naked. We all are, aside from Zaviar.

I can't help but remember how she trembled beneath me. And then how her eyes shined as she looked up at me like she wanted to say something.

What did she want to say?

"It's obvious. She wanted to cum," Krave says without thought.

All three of us slowly pan our attention to the incubus trailing his dark, glittering finger across her stomach. Damien is the only one who doesn't stare at the man like he's a total idiot. The incubus sketches a glittering heart over her stomach. It's adorable until he adds an entirely too realistic cock penetrating the heart, turning the soul into a pussy with just a few quick movements of his hand . . .

She shivers beneath his touch.

"You're a fuckin' dumbass," Zaviar tells him with absolutely no filter whatsoever.

Krave sweeps away his drawing and turns to the angel.

"Why? Because I don't want to tell you she's too afraid to change how things are?" Krave cocks a brow at the angel. They stare, slicing deadly daggers at one another.

And then we're all speechless.

"What do you mean?" Damien finally asks him and I see a curiousness in his brown eyes as he looks at Krave. I think it's the same curiousness he always has when it comes to this demon. He just isn't hiding it any more.

Krave lifts his inky fingers and smoke wafts out in thin-lined drawings. A lithe woman in glittering colors fans her dress out as she spins and shields four figures behind her.

She's beautiful. The way Krave sees her is different than how she looks. Aries is incredibly sexy, but the elegant lines Krave draws her in is all soft features and innocent eyes.

He sees her in a different light than the rest of the world does.

Maybe we all do.

"It's apparent, isn't it?" He cocks his head at me, but I just eye the incubus without a word until he explains further. "She figured out . . . whatever it she was trying to figure out. All the stuff she was working toward, she seemed to get it all sorted. And now she's hiding us away because the last time she made a big move, it nearly got us killed. It got you three imprisoned. She doesn't want to risk us. She knows as mates, we'd die for her." Krave lifts and looks around at the three of us like that should be obvious.

Fuck. It should be obvious.

"Well, we can't stay here. Her father wants an heir in his kingdom. It's safe for him if Aries is there." Zaviar rolls his bright eyes, and even in the moonlight, I can see his anger.

If he fucked her, would it wash away some of that hate? If he got just one thing that he wanted, would it change him?

Doubtful.

But judging from how much control he had tonight with her perfect body laid out before him and him still clinging to that restraint, maybe we'll never know.

"What do we do now?" Damien asks with his attention held on the woman at his side.

I've never seen someone love anyone so much in so little time.

Maybe that's what mating is like, though. I guess that's what love is like.

Love is patient.

It's fucked up, but it's patient.

And that's the answer here.

"We wait," I finally say, settling back against the netting and watching the night pass us by.

The moon hangs above with white slices of light casting across her features. Quiet snores catch the cool night air, and still I lie there awake, looking at her.

A beautiful woman is enough to cause so much violence from so many men. And us four, we have too much violence inside of us not to give it all up for her.

That's how I know Krave's right.

We would die for her.

CHAPTER SIXTEEN
Jizz Muffin
Aries

The blade cuts into his throat. Sure, it's wooden, and yeah, it's just a blunt edge against Damien's smooth golden skin, but it still makes me feel good to use my skills like I used to.

"Gods, put some strength into fending her off. Your big muscles look useless right now," Krave comments as he leans lazily against the training room wall. "Stop letting her win."

"I'm fucking notttt," Damien cuts out on a gargle of words.

"Oh. Well, in that case, perhaps go a bit easier on the poor guy, love." Krave's tone holds a slight worried edge, but the three men watching us never intervene.

His big hands fumble against my wrists, but he

hasn't said the safe word yet, either, so I keep my weapon in place. My hands hold the sword down firmly in place as his face turns a deeper shade. Almost red. My thighs shift against his smooth ribs and during this intense moment, I almost think about how he felt between my thighs earlier this morning.

Grinding and thrusting and making me wetter and wetter while the others slept.

I pull back. Just minimally. Just enough for air to hit his ragged lungs.

"Don't," Ryke warns.

He's so war-driven.

Krave's pleading me for kindness on his friend while Ryke's screaming for me to take his head clean off.

"Don't let up until he says it," Ryke instructs.

He's right.

Of course, he's right.

Orgasms mean nothing during battle.

After and before battle are a different story.

But for now.

"Just say it," I whisper, dipping my head low so my words fan against Damien's parted lips.

"Fuck, no." His jaw clenches but heaving breath exhales hard from his nose.

"Please." My lower lip juts out as I pout for him while strangling him slowly.

"No," Damien says against a rasping cough and a jagged breath.

My lips press to his, and though he can't find any air in the room, he still kisses me back. It makes me worried about his insanity that he puts lust above life in this moment.

"Say the words, Damien." I arch a brow at him as my lips hover over his.

His jaw steels once more before he gives in. "Fuck," he sighs defeatedly. "Jizz Muffin." The safe words are rasping and crackly, but it still makes Krave and Zaviar laugh.

Even Ryke smiles.

Even I smile.

Victory never sounded so sweet.

The moment I pull my wooden sword fully away, his fingers tangle through my damp hair, and he pulls me down to him, stealing my mouth for himself the moment I'm close enough. Damien kisses me hard, nipping at my lip, while something hard and telling presses against my core.

A moan pushes from my mouth at the feel of it, but more thoughts flutter through my mind as well.

. . . how is it that Krave's magic can dissolve Corva's and give Damien back what he lost? Krave's a demon . . . but his magic isn't dark and tainted like hers . . .

How—

"That's enough," a deep voice rumbles.

A foot presses against my side, and I roll out of Damien's warm touch as I lie back and stare up at the massive man smirking down on me.

"He can say he gave it his all, but I know he'd never hurt you. Mate magic is more powerful than anything. Wasn't a fair fight," Ryke says with a shake of his head.

"What do you suggest?" I don't move. I'm flat on my back, but I'll know the moment Ryke tries to strike. His muscles are powerful, sure, but they're telling. They flex and tense when he's about to go in for a blow. Not only that, but he's looking at me with too much kindness in his eyes.

"Fight Zaviar. Fight someone who isn't a puddle of love at your feet." Ryke turns to the man with the big pink wings looming over his dark serious features.

My gaze locks with his and though we haven't had sex, I can still hear his whispered confession ringing in my ears.

I love you so fuckin' much, Aries.

I shiver in response like I can still feel his breath against my skin.

He remains impassive. The deadness in his gaze is still there, and I start to wonder if he even remembers what he said at all.

Maybe he doesn't realize it was spoken out loud.

Maybe I should ignore it.

Maybe—

A fiery scent hits the air as sparking white color flashes across the blue mat. And then, a hard wooden sword cuts through the air. It's aimed straight for my face. I roll from beneath that swinging strike. Zaviar's teeth are still clenched together hard as I catch my wooden hilt in my hand and roll to a standing position.

"Still aren't used to that angel magic, are you?" Zaviar asks with a smirk.

"You're cute when you're mad, Remorseless," I tell him with my lips quirking at one side.

He sweeps his blade back and angles it out with a hard blow that hits my weapon with jolting force. That cocky smirk fades from his face.

"I fuckin' hate when you call me that." He seethes, our blades separating our warm breaths that clash together

154

between us. The two of us hold the pose there, neither of us giving in, even as our arms shake.

"Why. What does it mean? Tell me why you live without regret and without remorse," I ask, my finger slipping out and skimming quick over the tense muscles of his ribs. It's the faintest touch of my skin against his slick tattoos. Brief. Less than a second.

But I see the tremble that shakes through his body as he shoves off from my defense and circles the room to recompose.

Or to think through his next move.

Or maybe both.

His stride wavers with an arrogance of slow pent-up strength and dominance.

Too bad I can see how pissed off he is over one simple question.

"Tell me why I've been here for five godsdamn days with nothing better to do but watch you fuck my friends—and Krave—"

"Hey!" Krave answers, as if he's hurt from the sting of that separation.

"And I'll tell you why I hate that name you love so fuckin' much," Zav says with his deep blue eyes held hard on me.

I swallow when I realize what he wants.

I want more time, though. I want to clear my head. I want to rest before it all comes crashing down all over again.

My wings spread out wide, and with both hands on my hilt, I bring it downward, fast and spiraling.

Zaviar dodges the blow. His big arms wrap around me, and he slams me to the soft mat with so much force, my weapon rattles out of my hand. And it doesn't matter. Because his calloused fingers grip my wrists, and in the span of a single pounding heartbeat, he has my hands held above my head, his piercing eyes slicing right into me.

"Tell me, Crow," he demands. His bodyweight presses in to me just right.

I can't breathe. I can't catch my breath, and I can't think about all the things that are a chaotic swirl within my mind. It's too much. There's too much to say that I haven't said yet.

"Catherine's gone," I blurt. His dark lashes flutter, and his gaze softens as he watches me. "She's quiet, and she's emotionless, and I don't know if I lost her, or if . . ." I choke on those words, but there's so many more waiting to get out. "I don't want to murder my father. I want to kill the cruel racist fucking king, but I want to save my father, who sent me away to protect me, and I can't do both of those things when the two men are one and the same." Zaviar's hold on me loosens, but his warm hands never slip away from my arms. His fingers stroke back and forth as a shaking breath storms my lungs and even more words vomit from my mouth. "And I finally have four people who would protect me at all costs, who care about me more than anyone ever has, and I'm so fucking terrified I'll do to them what I've done to my mother. What I've done to the Shadow Guard. What I've done to myself." I close my eyes hard before the dampness there trails out.

Steady fingers push back my hair. My breathing stays reckless even as warm lips press at the corner of my lips. He kisses there before he leans in close, his breath skimming across my neck before he whispers in my ear.

"I—I hate when you call me Remorseless because ever since I left the gods, I regret so fuckin' much, it makes me hate myself more and more each day." His rumbling words are low and filled with . . . *remorse*. My wet lashes lift, and I lock eyes with deep dark blue ones. "Don't be like me, Pretty Crow. Don't regret the things you didn't do. Don't hide here and wait for shit to sort itself out. That's not you." His gaze slips to my parted lips for a second, filled with tension and heat.

And then he shoves off of me. He leaves me there on the floor as I stare up at the carved wooden beams of the ceiling above.

"Am I mistaken, or doesn't someone have safe words that must be said to end the sparring?" Krave asks quietly as Zaviar shoves open the door.

The angel glares back at the incubus from over his big pink wings.

"Fucking Jizz Muffin," Zaviar grumbles before the door shuts hard behind him.

The smiles aren't there this time. Only silence follows.

A bitter twisting sensation fills my stomach, and it makes me physically sick to think about what he told me.

And I hate that he's right.

CHAPTER SEVENTEEN
The Advisors
Aries

The sun burns behind the sharp peaks of the castle rooftops. I feel small at the base of it all, staring up at the smooth brick and inhaling the morning air that's tinged with red roses and bloody memories.

"We don't have to go in, love," Krave whispers at my side, his fingers lifted, but he never runs his distracting touch along my skin.

Zaviar clears his throat hard from behind me, but all four of the men just let me keep my quiet. For just a few seconds longer.

Just a little while.

"Your father's looking for you," a breathless voice calls as Nille runs through the rose garden, his little feet rushing despite how slow the goblin is actually moving.

"Your mother said to keep your absence a secret, but your father hasn't stopped screaming about it for days now." His big head bobs as the height of the bushes nearly overtakes him.

"Thank you, Nille," I call after him.

A calmer presence steps forward in a deep red gown that matches the feathers that span around her slender frame.

Nille scuttles to a stop on the dirty brick sidewalk and stares up at his Queen.

She seems so tall and powerful in comparison to the goblin. She hasn't seemed that way in my eyes for years.

The three demons and the angel all shift closer to me. They linger on shifting feet as if my mother alone in her garden is a threat to me.

"I always told your father you were the good one," she says on a whisper so quiet, it barely kisses the breeze. "I always reminded him that you were different. That you needed time to grow out of childish thoughts, and I always asked him to show our sweet girl kindness." She doesn't look at me as she says it all. "As you grew older, I saw your recklessness, and I thought it made you stronger, even if it was a dangerous trait." Her eyes close hard, and when she opens them, she's staring daggers into my soul. "I didn't know it made you deadly. I didn't know—" A gasping breath shoves from her lungs. Her emotions snap, and she's composed so quickly, my trembling heart doesn't know how to react to my mother, who's always so calm, it's hard to process all of this. "I love you, but do not harm him, Ari. Everything that's ever been cast upon him, all magic good and bad, will be inherited by you. You don't know what hell he has hanging over his head." Her eyes hold mine, and I wish like fuck I could tell her that I do.

I *do* know what hell is hanging over his head, because that hell has made a home inside my head for the last three fucking years.

I nod to her slowly, and she simply walks away. I don't know what I'm nodding about because I honestly can't agree to what she just asked of me. I can't say I won't kill him.

I can only promise to keep her and this kingdom safe.

One way or another.

***

Three men file into the room with smiles on their faces for their weekly meeting. Those smiles fall one by one as they each take sight of me sitting in my father's chair at the far end of the table. I also note the way their attention rakes over the four men standing behind me.

"Good morning," I say loudly, chin angling up to meet each of their gawking stares.

"Where is King Gravier?" Johnn asks, taking the seat on my right-hand side.

Johnn, my new right-hand man.

Just the man, I know, who can help all of the pieces fall into place.

"He told me last week he advised you that I would be filling a few of his less urgent rolls within the castle, Sir Johnn," I say with a tilt of my head.

"I—he—I don't recall that conversation. I'll have to reassess my notes, I suppose," Johnn says with flawless recovery. Very well done for a man who wanted to put the blame on his king, which we all know, that is not a thing in these castle walls.

And that is why it'll make my plan so easy to shove into place.

"The King told us you'd run off somewhere during the last six days." The older gentleman, Waltry, at the end of the table, narrows his eyes on me.

He's the oldest of the three men. He's so old, he was Hyval's advisor when she was Queen. He'll either be the hardest to break, or the easiest.

Depending on how much he fears his mortality. Because he's seen all of this once before. During my grandmother's reign.

Will he stand to see it all again?

I, too, send him a questioning stare right back as I shake my head slowly.

"No. I'm sorry. Please allow me to apologize on my father's behalf. He sent me to ask the King's Mother about the technique of memory stones. I'm not sure how he wants us to use them, but they are indeed very interesting sources of magic," I say with forced enthusiasm dripping from my smiling lips.

Waltry's gray eyebrows lift as he stares at me as if he's seen a ghost.

"Memory stones," Waltry whispers.

I nod with a smile.

"Surely, he's told you. It would be odd of my father not to have a very informed group of advisors advising him." I cock my head and wait for someone to dare say the King never mentioned it.

I can lead a horse to water, but I can't make him say shit against his King, now, can I?

Johnn is the only man in the room with the brain to

stall the conversation. "I'm sure it's in my notes, Princess Aries." His smile is kind as he looks my way and begins pulling a paper from his folder.

Pen steps quietly into the room. Her gaze watchful, but her mouth sealed tightly shut.

"There is an urgent matter for the . . . royal house to decide on." Johnn's dark eyes scan his papers.

"*The King*. It's for the King to decide on, Sir Johnn," the man to my left, the one with the stern features, cuts in before Johnn can hand the wafting white page to me.

I don't know this one. He's old, with only a few gray hairs left on his balding head, but he wasn't here when I was here years ago.

My fingers remain clamped with tension in my knuckles to keep me from ripping the page from the poor man's hand.

"The King requested Aries handle today's meeting. I apologize if it slipped his mind,' Pen says without blinking at the men staring at her.

She's confident. Perfectly confident.

Even for a liar.

"The King . . . is out at the moment. It couldn't hurt for Princess Aries to step in. As the King said she would," Johnn says carefully.

The guy with the stick up his ass shakes his head hard. His lips purse even more, and I swear, he must have licked a lemon right out of someone's asshole before he got here.

"Actually," Waltry says with a hesitant tone lacing that one promising word. Make or break it, Walt. Do it. Do it now! "I think in light of the king's recent absentmindedness; we should reschedule today's meeting until after he's advised us further."

Fuck!

Come on, Walt! You were supposed to be on my side.

You saw what happened to Grandmother Hyval, and the slow downward spiral her life took! And you're willing to do it again?

I swallow hard but never drop my smile as I release the paper so hard, it flits out of Johnn's fucking hand.

"Of course," I smooth my dress and sweetly look from one man to the next before saying what my father always did. "You're dismissed, gentlemen."

Old Stick Up His Ass does not like that.

He's not going to enjoy what I have planned next.

Not one bit.

CHAPTER EIGHTEEN
A Favor
Damien

"Do you think the game she's playing is dangerous for her?" I ask Zaviar as we trail quietly behind the Princess, who smiles at everyone she passes.

It's like she's an entirely different person right now.

"Everything in Aries's life is dangerous for her." Zaviar gives a maid a curled lip glare as he passes, and she scurries even faster down the corridor.

"Do you have to look like that?" My eyes roll as a heavy sigh shoves from my lungs.

Everyone's exhausting today.

"Like what?" My brother has the audacity to ask with that same eat-shit-and-die look on his face.

"Never mind."

"Let him pout," Krave says, as his arm brushes my side. A tingling sensation races across my skin at the simple feel of his arm against mine.

I blink the distracting thoughts away and focus on the woman ahead of me.

We all do. Ryke's the only one not concerned with wherever the hell we're going now.

In fact—

The demon cuts in front of Aries and sweeps open the left-hand door for her. Aries smiles up at him as she slips inside.

Then he, too, strides in like he's been here his whole life.

"Ryke! I missed—where have you been?" The young blonde girl, Pen, asks, her cheeks tinting a strange color of pink when she looks at Ryke with stars in her eyes.

Seriously, what is with everyone today?

"Uncle Gravier has been asking about Ari," the girl keeps rambling. On and on about how we've all missed events here and there, and the king's made excuses all over.

And still Aries just stares at her with that deranged smile on her face.

Until the girl shuts the fuck up about the king.

Finally.

"I think you should have Ryke. I see the way you look at him and the way he looks at you," Pen says on a new topic that makes Ryke's mouth drop open slowly.

But it isn't one Aries wants to talk about right now.

"You lied for me," Aries says flatly.

The smile falls from the girl's soft features.

"I need a favor, Pen," Aries adds, like she's watched

166

one too many mafia movies back in the Bin.

Pen looks around at all of us one by one, and I try my best to feign interest in her frilly white curtains on the far side of the bedroom. They match her white bedspread. Everything is crisp and perfect in this room.

Just like the young girl staring up at the Princess.

"What do you need?" The moment Pen asks it, Krave shuts the door.

The click of the lock should be alarming when surrounded by so many powerful people in such a small space.

But the girl's features remain smooth. She's . . . very composed, if nothing else. Royals seem incredibly good at constraining their emotions at all costs. False calm is their forte.

They're just as bad as Krave.

And now, I see it up close and personal between the two women currently playing the game among themselves.

"Reschedule my father's weekly meetings." Long silver hair fans over the small of Aries back as she tilts her head at the girl.

"Okay," Pen says slowly.

"And then don't tell my father."

"Why?" Pen's false calm is now slightly less calm.

She's not as good at the game as Aries, it seems.

"There are people in this kingdom who want to kill our King, Pen. Not everyone thinks like him. Not everyone despises demons the way he does. And not everyone wants their future to be his." Aries's words are spoken honestly and flawlessly, and they seem to give Pen a hard line between her eyebrows as she looks at the Princess.

"I know," Pen says quietly. "Are you—is *someone* planning to kill King Gravier?"

The carefulness of this conversation is astounding.

Ryke sighs impatiently, while Krave just watches with that glinting look in his depthless eyes. When I glance to Zaviar, his hand is hovering over his heart. And his jaw is clenched so hard, he's sweating.

He's in pain. *Again*. And he's too much of a hardass to admit it.

I shake my head at the asshole and keep my silence.

"At the moment, no one is taking action to kill him," Aries says as her voice drops to a mere whisper. "But I'd like it to not come to that. To keep him safe, I'd like to take over for him."

Careful, careful, Aries.

"You want to become Queen?" Pen asks, hissing the words out on a whisper that slithers around the room.

Aries swallows hard and takes a breath before answering.

"I don't *want* to be Queen. I need to be. To keep demons safe. To keep my father safe. And to keep the people of this kingdom safe." A tired breath slips from Aries's lips, and it's just now that I realize how much she's carrying around at all times. She's tired. But she's still trying. "So. Will you do me a favor, Pen?"

The two girls stare at one another. The shape of their eyes and the sharp angle of their chins are so similar. The two of them seem more similar than either of them ever realized.

"Just tell me what you need, and I'll do it, Aries," Pen says with a small lift of her chin.

Loyal.

They're both unbelievably loyal, it seems.

I just hope the young girl isn't as reckless as Aries.

The world can't handle two Aries Sinclaires, that's for damn sure.

CHAPTER NINETEEN
Diplomatic Ducks
Aries

I've met my father's assessing stares for two days now. He hasn't asked where I was. He hasn't welcomed me back. He hasn't much spoken to me at all, really.

He just watches.

I bet he wishes he had another fated mate to spy on me now.

None of it matters. Because today is the day I break the trust between him and his advisors.

The meeting room door swings open without a sound, and once more, those charming men walk in with laughter and smiles.

And once more, those smiles fall to the floor when they spot me.

And then Pen, who stands quietly behind me.

"Princess Aries. Good morning," Johnn says with genuine politeness.

I like Johnn. He's smart. Plus, he wants what I want. He just doesn't have the fae balls to say it out loud.

"Morning, gentlemen."

Old Stick Up His Ass full on grimaces.

Lovely.

"Good morning, Princess Aries," Waltry says with a low bow that displays his graying hair.

We have two out of three on my side. Ish.

We also have Pen, which is immensely helpful to get that third duck in line.

"Will your father be joining us this morning, or will this prove to be another utter waste of time?" Ass Stick drones with heavy brows shadowing his dark eyes.

Fucking duck.

"Sir Timmons, I sent you a formal notice that King Gravier wishes for Aries to lead these meetings from now on in his absence," Pen says swiftly like my ever-saving grace.

Sir Timmons-Ass Stick eyes the young girl.

Silence passes during this long, drawn-out show.

"It was signed in his pen, Sir," Pen adds with a smile.

Wow. She forges signatures now.

What monster have I created?

"Princess, I do apologize. Please tell us what the agenda meant when it said 'health conditions'." Johnn's smile could melt hearts.

Sweeter hearts. More innocent hearts—I pause my thoughts, and when I glance back at Pen, she's blushing.

Ah, there's the sweet innocent heart.

Johnn doesn't peer back at my cousin at all, though.

He's too focused.

Which is good. That's his job, after all.

"What I am about to say does not leave this room, gentlemen." I pass my gaze over one man and then the next. They all nod. Aside from Timmons, but fuck a duck, this is sink-or-swim, and if I have to drown one fucking dawdling duck, so be it. "My father's memory isn't what it used to be."

Waltry's throat works as he swallows hard. His eyes now wider with the information he clearly suspected just days ago.

"We're all a bit forgetful in our old age. It isn't something to clutter up meetings over," Timmons groans.

"Sir, please let her finish," Johnn says.

"Finish what?" Timmon's voice booms through the long room. "Finish wasting my time? Wasting this kingdom's time? In all my years—"

"Her father's mother has a history of Degenerative Remembrance, Timmons!" Waltry yells. His jaw clamps shut before he spews more than just information at the man seated next to him.

"*Memory fleet,*" Timmons says on a wavering whisper.

My gaze flits down to the glossy tabletop, and my big silver eyes stare back at me as I hang my head low.

"Aries," Johnn whispers, his palm held just slightly over mine. "I'm sorry if Sir Timmons upset you, Princess. He won't say another word."

My lashes flutter up just in time to spot Johnn cocking a brow at the man across from him in the sternest brow cocking I've ever seen.

Tension slips into the room.

"I—I apologize, Princess. I did not know," Timmons apologizes on a quiet but steady tone.

"He's sick," I say on my smallest voice, my lip wobbling dramatically. "I just want to protect him. I want to take care of him while he still remembers me." I blink away the sudden wetness in my eyes, and it's odd how hard it hits home for me.

Not for my father.

But for Hyval. No one took care of her. She tried to take care of herself. She tried so hard to keep her life together when no one was there to help her.

She and I are alike.

Except I have men who love me.

And they'll never understand how much they mean to me.

I swallow hard, and it's then that I realize how much of a twist my dramatic acting has shifted into real-life emotions.

Fuck.

"The King wanted to bring the kingdom together for a memorial for his son. He wanted a speech to be given," Pen says, and I swivel in my chair to look at her.

That was not on the fucking script, Pen!

She ignores my wide-eyed stare, though.

Another party? For the brother I killed?

"The King isn't in a position to give speeches," Waltry warns flatly.

To my surprise, Timmons nods in agreement.

Look at how my little duck has found his place in line.

"I think . . . I think it might be best if Aries was a sort

174

of . . . speaker for the King," Johnn suggests with a mixture of confidence and caution.

My brows lift. It's candid shock. Because quite honestly, who fucking knew it was this easy to take over a kingdom?

"I agree. Let's schedule the memorial for late this week, but the King is not to address the public," Waltry says severely, and I can't help but smile at my secret triumph. "Aries will give the speech."

My smile falls flat on the floor as I imagine the speech I could give for the man I murdered.

Fucking lovely.

CHAPTER TWENTY
The Love in Lust
Aries

It's heart stoppingly terrifying how real a simple dream can feel.

Even if you know it's just a dream.

Long fingers slide over mine just as they did once before. He claws at me for the tiny vial in my hand. The darkness of her tomb envelopes us, but I'll always remember the feel of his nails scraping over my skin.

"Give me the ashes, Aries!" Nathiale screams at me, and his words carry on, racing over the walls of the solid brick room.

"Fuck you." My fist collides with his nose, and I feel the warmth of his blood across my knuckles.

His head cracks against the pedestal that once held the demonic vial that's fisted in my sweaty hand. He's down, but his fingers dig into my boot in a matter of half a second. He's dragging me down and clawing up my body.

It won't stop. Neither of us will give in until one of us is dead.

Unless.

My thumb pushes off the cork, and the scent of embers fills my nostrils.

And then it literally *fills my nostrils*. I lift the small vial up close and personal until it drags over my upper lip.

I breathe in hard through my nose. My body attempts to cough it out involuntarily, but I feel it. It courses through my lungs and even farther. It's a chaotic tornado within my veins. It's a swirl of dust within my mind. It's everywhere.

It consumes me.

Nathiale tears the empty bottle from my hands in the dense darkness and gives me a swift kick to my ribs as I continue dry heaving at his feet.

"Thank you, sister." I can hear the sneer on his lips. The victory in his voice is hard to miss.

He's going to be fucking furious when he realizes what I've taken from him.

He'll kill me for this when he sees the empty glass vial.

But I'm calm as I lie there. I'm calm because somewhere, at the back of my mind, I know this is all in the past. And I know what lies in Nathiale's future.

I know my father will banish me from his kingdom before the sun rises. I can almost hear the worry in his tone from all those years ago.

This is all just a dream.

"What kind of monster kills someone so violently,

Aries?" Nathiale asks.

The darkness presses in on me.

I—I don't remember this.

Did he really say that?

"You hit me so hard with the crown, you cracked my skull with the first blow. But you kept going until my blood painted your hands, Aries." His voice slithers over me.

A tremble shakes down my spine.

"What are you talking about?" I finally ask.

A hue of soft golden light strikes up at the center of the room, just over the vial's black pedestal. Its light spider-walks across the small room, lighting up what I've never laid eyes on in my entire life.

My heart drills in my chest.

The light crawls farther and farther.

And then my brother's bloody, disfigured face is looking down on me. Flesh and hair hangs from his features, twisting his once-handsome appearance into something grotesque and unnerving.

"You want to know why Catherine left you? It's not because you're stronger now, Aries. It's because you're dangerous. You hurt her. You hurt me. You hurt everyone around you, sister," he says through split swollen lips.

"Shut up." I shove to my feet, but when I stand, I can't take another step. My feet are glued to the dark, brick floor.

"Maybe I will. Maybe I'll just shut up." He tilts his mangled head at me. "I'll let you talk for a while. Maybe . . . maybe you should say something nice about me."

I blink at him, and the twisting feeling in my stomach lurches a little harder. "What?"

"Say. Something. Nice. About your dear, sweet, *dead* brother, Aries."

Fuck.

He continues in that seething, roaring voice of his that scuttles over the walls and echoes into my chest. "Tell everyone. Tell them how you hated me, even when we were children. Tell them how you fantasized about burying me alive in our sandbox. Or pushing me down mother's stairs. Or shoving a pillow over my face until I couldn't breathe or speak any longer. Tell them that fond memory, Aries. Tell them. Tell them. Tell them!"

The memorial . . .

My eyes flash open with the whooshing sound of my pulse filling my ears. Trembling breaths shake across my lips, and I just stare up at the shadows along the ceiling with the image of his face burned into my mind.

Warm fingers slide over my stomach, slow but soothing.

Ryke pulls me hard against his big chest, and the men around me in bed are fast asleep. I settle in against his warmth, but my eyes refuse to close. I can't sleep. All I can think about is that fucked-up dream and the fucked-up things I'll have to say tomorrow night at the memorial.

An hour slips by into the silence. My thoughts are no lighter, but my eyes feel heavier. They close slowly. Sleep touches around the edges of my mind. Peace settles into my chest.

I open my eyes once more.

Movement outside the glass balcony doors catches my attention. Translucent black hair flicks across her pale features, and the woman taps ever-so-lightly against the glass.

If my fucking siblings could let me rest for a single hour, I would be so appreciative.

Unfortunately, Corva continues to rap against the balcony door like a fly buzzing around my face, until I'm forced to throw my feet over the edge of the bed. The thin black nightgown flits around my thighs, and I'm already huffing out a breath of frustration before I even storm across the room and throw open the doors.

"What?" I hiss through my teeth. The cold wind catches at my hair and clothes, but the woman in front of me seems unaffected.

"How's the angel?"

"Are you fucking kidding me? He's fantastic. Good night, Corva."

"Then pardon me."

"Pardon you? Pardon me." I throw the words back in her face, and it only makes her eyes blaze larger.

"I mean, pardon my banishment. Only a royal of the Kingdom of Roses can welcome me back. Welcome me back, Aries." Inky hair flicks over her pale features.

My heart kicks up all over again with rapid apprehension.

"Not tonight."

"Tonight!"

"No. It's incredibly bad timing." I try to plot my next moves. After the party, after I show the crowd my father's inability to rule, after I've been crowned and the kingdom is safe, then it would be safe for Corva as well.

But not tonight.

"Aries. Fae do not give something for nothing,"

Corva says in a cutting tone I've heard her use a time or two before.

It's eerie and singed in the natural dark power that courses through her bones.

"And I keep my word. I'll bring you back to court. I can't pardon you tonight, though. There's too much riding on tomorrow, Corva." I tip my chin up slowly and hold the edgy gaze of my older sister.

A beat passes between our held stares.

"Tomorrow, then." She, too, tips her head up with composure. "Tomorrow at midnight."

I nod slowly.

"Say it, Aries."

I swallow slowly, and it only makes my heart pound harder when I've been given a time limit. A deadline. A fucking execution date.

"Tomorrow. At midnight. I pardon the banishment of Corva of the Unknown at midnight of tomorrow eve," I say with as much etiquette as I can muster.

A soft smile curls her lips.

"Thank you," she whispers.

Her hand reaches out to clutch mine.

But a flash of light shields her touch. Her fingers dip ripples into the unseen barrier that separates her from me. It separates her from her home.

And I know what that feels like.

Her smiles wavers, but just as our mother taught us, she lifts her head high and pulls away from me. She nods as though she's about to say her goodbye.

I don't know why it hurts my heart to see someone go through what I've been through.

It didn't used to.

I can't explain it.

At the last second, just before her wafting black wings sweep her away, I step forward. I walk across whatever line that says she's not welcome here, and I wrap my arms around my sister in a way that I haven't done since I was a little girl.

Slender shoulders stiffen against my embrace. Her heartbeat pounds against mine for several seconds before her thin arms slowly slip around me. And then she hugs me so hard, it wells up emotion deep in my chest. Emotions I didn't realize I held for her.

We're sisters.

She isn't kind, and she isn't perfect. But neither am I. And neither of us want the future our family has tried to thrust us into.

"Whatever you're worried about, you'll do great, Aries." Her tone is steady and sure.

I wish I fucking was.

"Thanks," I whisper, before untangling myself from her slender frame.

"I'll see you tomorrow," she says with a nod.

"Yeah. See you tomorrow," I repeat, just as a puff of black smoke erupts.

Then she's gone.

She's so set on tomorrow. And I'll keep my word.

Unless my plan is shit. And father banishes my ass to the Torch this time, instead of the Bin.

At least I'd be with my mates, though.

A strange calm descends through me at that thought. I'll have them. I won't be alone. Maybe everything will go perfectly tomorrow, but even if it doesn't, we'll always be together.

I turn and close the door quietly behind me, but I stand there in the darkness. A tangle of strong arms and muscled thighs are all I see on the large bed, and my heart warms as I study them.

"I'm told it's weird to watch someone sleep, love," Krave says from the far side of the large king-size mattress.

"I'm pretty sure *I* told you that." I fold my arms, and it's then that all four of them shift beneath the white sheets.

I woke them up. And no one's complaining about it . . .

My bare feet are quiet as I pad back over to the bed that has far too many men in it. Or maybe just enough.

My palms sink into the soft mattress, and my knees follow, as I climb up the center of where they sleep. Feet and legs slide out of my way. One leg, however, slips over to get in my way. Or to lead me up a hard, beautiful body.

My hands settle on either side of lean, narrow hips before trailing up the rest of the way.

I shouldn't be surprised to be looking down on the most beautiful warm brown eyes.

His big hands skim up my thighs, fingers teasing along the hem of the nightgown as I straddle my thighs over his stomach. A sexy smile pulls at his lips as I lower fully against him. He pushes my thighs until I shift lower. Our hips line up just where he wants me. He likes me like this. He likes holding me and guiding me as I fuck him.

It's . . . empowering in a way.

So empowering that I lean over him and slide my fingers down the lines of Zaviar's chest as I grind ever so lightly against Damien.

Deep intense eyes study me as he sits up in bed. Zaviar's dark lashes lower, and I feel his apprehension as he looks from one person to the next. His head dips, and I lean into his intoxicating mouth.

But he angles his head, and presses a kiss to the corner of my parted lips. "Goodnight, Pretty Crow," he whispers against my cheek.

Then he shoves off the mattress, climbs over Ryke, and gets out of bed. My mouth's still open as I watch him grab his jeans from the floor.

No one says a word as the pounding of my heart becomes painful. It hurts even more as he opens the door.

And walks out.

Damien sits up with hesitation strung through his taut shoulders. His chest skims mine just as big hands clasp my jawline, and he forces me to look at him.

"He doesn't want to hurt you," he whispers on a quiet tone and a soft kiss to my lips. He presses another chaste kiss there again and again. "He's an asshole, but he cares about you. And he doesn't want it to hurt any more than it already does when he has to leave."

Those soft-spoken words only slice open my heart even more.

When he has to leave.

I'm not an idiot. I know he'll leave. I know he can't stay. I've told myself the same thing a thousand times. But . . . it's harder to hear the words spoken out loud.

My hands fall between us, and Damien stops the slow press of his lips against mine.

Someone else isn't as easily convinced of my

determination to wallow in my self-pity, though.

Strong arms with etching veins and deeper etching scars wrap around my stomach with a soft sting of iron washing over my flesh. He's careful with the slicing weapons cutting through his forearms, but it doesn't stop him from holding me from behind.

"You should relax for a while," Ryke whispers along my ear, a breath of rasping words that shiver all through me.

His hand slides lower down my abdomen.

"Do you want to lie down, or do you want us to take care of you, or both?" Ryke asks attentively, and it knocks the air right from my lungs with the idea of what he's suggesting.

"Both is nice," a voice at my side purrs.

I catch the devilish eyes of the sexy incubus who's now completely naked, and I'm not sure when he took off his jeans, but they're off and he's . . . incredibly ready. My fingers lift casually, and I skim along the hard length of Krave's cock as I hold his gaze.

His lashes flutter with lust in his gaze, and before I even reply, he tangles his hand through my hair and pulls me hard against his lips. His tongue slides over mine before our lips fully meet, and a low groan hums through the room from the two men surrounding us. I dive into the feel of his hands tingling across my skin, and the desire he spreads through me.

I get lost in him entirely.

Until the sound of metal skittering over metal draws my attention. I pull back just in time to see Ryke pulling the curtains closed over the balcony doors. I watch with heavy breaths leaving my lungs as he does the same thing at one window. Then the next.

Until complete darkness caresses me.

"Lie back," Krave says on a low, sex-filled voice.

Damien's palms brush up and down my thighs once more, then his warm touch slips away. No one touches me, so I do as I'm told and slide over Damien's hips and shift against the soft blankets until my head meets the fluffy pillow. In the darkness, I lie perfectly still at the edge of the bed. I feel every breath of air hit my lungs, and I'm all too aware of the anticipating way my hearts pounding into my chest.

Gentle hands slide over my silk night gown. Up, up, up they trail. A big hand cups my breast, and my breath catches as warmth sears over the material. It's a faint touch first. But then his mouth takes as much of me as he can, kissing and sucking and making my legs shake around total nothingness.

On my other side, a singeing palm is feather-light as it skims up my inner thigh. Another hand takes the same path up the sensitive flesh with sparking sensations kissing my skin as both of them glide toward the same spot at the center of my body. They meet, their fingers sliding together at the same time beneath my panties, and I can't stop my spine from arching up off the bed as their addictive touch slams waves of pulsing energy through my clit. They do it over and over and over again, until I'm crying out just from the light teasing of their hands and mouths alone.

At some point, as the room is shaking around me, and my head's thrust back into the pillow, someone parts my legs farther. He spreads me wide and demandingly, in a way that I'm not sure at all who it is.

Even as the smooth head of his dick skims along the fingers working my clit and glides over my entrance. Powerful hands shove my gown up around my stomach, and his palms grip me tightly as he slides in ever-so-slowly with a growling groan shaking from his chest.

Ryke?

He takes his time pumping into me, sliding along my sex just right, until it makes me crazy with how hard he's thrusting and how slow he's fucking. There's a current of fingers and tingling energy swirling through me from so many people caressing me at once. I can't distinguish one touch from another. I grip his wrists, sliding my fingers along the smooth skin of his forearms, his biceps, his shoulders, his strong, perfect jawline. And then I bring him down against me.

Soft lips press to mine. He tastes me with affection and leisurely flicks of his tongue. When we kiss, when light shines through me from his gentle affection alone, I know who it is.

"*Damien*," I whisper against his tongue, and he hums a delicious sound of approval as he kisses me deeper, fucks me deeper, takes me deeper on so many levels.

My leg slides higher against his, and we're a tangle of desire that just slams into me on vibrating waves right through my core until it busts. The air catches in my lungs as I throw my head back, and everything in me comes to life just for him with a shattering release that takes my breath away.

He kisses the exposed column of my neck as he fucks me harder, taking from me what he just gave, until everything in him matches everything in me. The muscles of

188

his arms are taut around me as he groans a gravelly sound along my throat, making me feel his release in the simple sound of his pleasure.

I press my lips to his, kissing him and breathing him in, just before his fingers dig into the curve of my ass, and he rolls us, bringing me down on top of him as he rocks his hips against mine. He starts all over again, just like that.

Just. Like. That.

"Don't be a greedy fuck," Ryke says, his low tone whispering around the room from somewhere nearby.

Steady palms brush over my hips with a faint caress of hands that shivers through me. He holds me sweetly from behind while Damien fucks me from below. The man behind me doesn't wait, though.

He grips my hips firmly, and slides Damien from me with one hard jerk.

A frustrated growl comes from my sweet mate as I land in front of him on all fours on the tangle of soft blankets. I can't tell if the hands holding my hips are singing with a light burn or singing with a static feel of incubus lust . . . both seem the same when there's an ache pulsing between my thighs.

Ryke . . . or Krave . . .

Long fingers follow the curve of my body from behind before dipping down at my center and gliding over my sex so slowly.

"He took care of you. Fucked you good, didn't he, love?" a rasping voice asks, drunken with need.

Krave.

His fingers slip into me, curving just right as he massages me slowly. My lashes flutter, and I don't know how, but he knows my body better than I do. I rock against his hand while his other palm trails down my spine. Sparking sensations follow his touch, and I gasp so loudly, I can practically hear him smirk.

Without a word, he pulls his hand back, leaving me with a cutting breath of disappointment falling from my lips. But he's right back against me in seconds. The smooth head of his cock teases my clit as he thrusts back and forth but never enters me.

He does it over and over again as I gasp each time he hits the right spot. It's heart-pounding perfection. But it's fleeting.

It's fucking torture.

"Krave," I whisper on a cry as he glides against me once more.

"Mmm, I love when you say my name like that." And then he slams into me so hard I lurch forward against Damien.

His nails bite into my skin while his hips drive in harder and harder. The feel of his magic collides within me from his touch alone, and the combination of that and how fast he's thrusting into my wetness crashes all the emotions inside me together.

I cum in seconds.

I'm a trembling, moaning mess in his hands, and his satisfaction is apparent when he hums a salacious rasp of a groan.

But he never slows.

My sex clenches around him again and again with an uncontrollable release washing through me for so long, it's like a high of dangerous desire.

He never cums. He slows. He takes his time drawing lines over my skin with his long fingers, until he finally pulls out. His incredible hardness skims along my thighs as I lie on my stomach in a heap of shuddering breaths and weak limbs.

"Go take a break, love," he says sweetly. "Then come back."

Come back . . . and sleep?

Doubtful.

Big hands scoop me up and wrap my legs around him, my head settling against the strong shoulder of whoever is carrying me. Exhaustion pulls at my shoulders, and I just want to stay in his arms forever.

"You tired, baby?" Ryke asks on a soft tone.

I nod, and he stands there in the dark, holding me in his arms, and I realize he doesn't want to put me down. His hands are high on my thighs, so, so close to my sex.

He's so big. Unbreakable. His body and his will.

"You're so sexy, Ryke," I whisper as I study the shadows of his face.

I can't see a single thing about him.

But fuck, he's so perfect. Gentle. Sweet. Powerful and deadly. Perfect.

A quiet laugh slips from his lips.

"What?" I ask, my fingers trailing along his coarse beard.

His head shakes back and forth beneath my touch. "You don't have to say that, Crow."

My head tilts ever so slightly. "What do you mean?"

He holds me closer in his arms, and I'm suddenly no longer tired. Nothing could wake me up more than the hanging silence Ryke is clinging to right now.

"I mean . . . I'm not attractive. I wasn't attractive as a Valkyrie, and I'm definitely not any better as one of your sister's fucked-up monsters."

My brows pull together hard as my heart dips in my chest.

"Your smile is pretty," I say like a blushing school girl, and his lips twitch up against my fingertips. "You're holding me here like I weigh nothing. That's sexy. Your resilient power, that's sexy. Your determination. Sexy. These," I run my fingers down the scarred lines of his rock-hard abdomen, "Maybe no one's told you, but these are sexy, Ryke." My hand slips between us, and my fingers curl around his member that's so thick, I can't wrap my hand fully around him. "This—this is so fucking sexy, Ryke," I say with a smile as I kiss him so slowly, his dick pulses in my palm.

"Yeah?" he asks with a smile that I kiss over and over again.

"That's enough of the pleasant small talk. Either fuck her or give her back," Krave says from behind us.

I lift in Ryke's arms, and he watches me in the darkness as I ever-so-slowly guide his thickness against my sex. Inch by inch, I take my time gliding down his shaft, and without breath in my lungs, I can hear every hard-cutting inhale he takes.

It's empowering sensuality.

My hips rock against his, and he meets every languid thrust I give. We cling to one other, breathing in the shaking breaths lingering between us as we steal away the sounds each of us gives up to one another. Sex with Ryke feels like being kissed by the sweet heavens while being fucked by the darkness of hell.

When I grind against the head of his cock before sliding down once more, he takes two big steps, and I'm slammed against a wall that rattles with picture frames. His pace turns lashing. Faster and faster, he drills into me. My nails sink into his skin just as sharp teeth drag over my throat, biting hard before sucking even harder.

The sensations climb together so high, I can't contain them.

And they spiral out of control when he sinks in as far as he can go, filling me so deeply, emotions burst inside of me in trembling waves that pulse all through my body.

The sound of my shaking moans echo around the room, and it just fuels him on. Faster and faster and faster until finally, he stills.

His big shoulders are rigid beneath my touch as he groans harshly against my neck in a way that feels animalist and delicious.

Silence settles around us. He slides out of me as he kisses the spot just beneath my ear with tender care. It's chaste, and it's sweet, and it makes me wonder . . . if he feels the torrent of energy that always surrounds us when we're like this.

Does he know?

I peer at him, but the shadows steal away the emotion on our faces.

He doesn't.

He doesn't know, because he has too much magic in his veins. There's already powerful energy in him at all times. It probably makes it impossible for him to feel the gentle tug of two hearts sealing together.

So he may never know what I know in this moment.

He's my mate.

They all are.

CHAPTER TWENTY-ONE
Forever Yours
Aries

The euphoric bliss I had last night is nowhere to be found today.

"I'd say red roses," my mother tells the castle florist. "Nathiale was pure like our kingdom's roses."

I close my eyes hard to stop myself from giving the world record for most epic eye roll. Pen arches a pale brow at me, but we both remain silent at the empty dinner table. Once again, three demons and a pink-feathered angel stand behind me. Zaviar hasn't said a word to me all day, and it's just one more thing I've tossed onto the anxiety pile that I'm carrying around this evening.

"Or maybe white. White symbolizes purity," Mother whispers just as the florist starts to walk away with her long list my mother gave her.

The pretty demon woman looks up at my mother hesitantly. Her brows lift high enough to almost touch her black horns among her deep purple hair.

She wants to go. She needs to hurry off and get an entire party thrown together in the next two hours.

And here we sit trying to decide if red or white flowers best represent a destructive fae fucker like Nathiale Sinclaire.

I say absolutely nothing.

Mother will never take my word of advice. Even if she has been giving me more worried glances since I left the castle without telling anyone.

She may worry about me, but she still isn't good at talking to me. Not after what I've done.

So I can only wait.

And wait.

And wait.

"Perhaps we'll do both and honor him with as many roses as our kingdom possesses." Pen suggests with a sweet smile on her lips.

The pale features on my mother's face soften as she gazes at my cousin. "You're right. We'll do both." She nods with a bit of finality, and I'm tempted to hug my quick-thinking cousin right on the spot.

But we have more important things to discuss.

"Why isn't Gravier here?" The royal woman at the end of the table cuts her attention to me with the intense suspicion only a queen is capable of.

It's only the three of us, my mates—plus Zav—and Nille.

"He's with his healer but should arrive tonight in

time for the memorial," I say with a lift of my chin, embodying total confidence.

I hope.

"Good," she says. She says it like she needs him. My mother's the most powerful woman I know. She's never needed my father for anything.

Except for this, it seems.

With the loss of her child, she's not as strong. Or maybe that's not it at all. Maybe it's the loss of a child, at the hands of a child . . . And now she has to look that child dead in the face every fucking day and pretend it's alright.

I can't change what I did, but I can change the hell we're all living in.

I can change the way we pretend.

That's what we do here in these castle walls. We walk among all the bad, all the hate, all the torment. And pretend everything is completely fine.

That's going to stop.

Tonight.

***

Soft violins drip sounds of sadness with every note they play. My gown is the same dark shade of ebony as my mother's. The room is a sea of fae dressed in shadowy gray-and-black colors. It makes it easy for Sev and Isabella to blend in with them.

But I do spot them. Watching me from the corner at the back of the ballroom.

Portraits of my brother line the walls, with soft golden candlelight casting out the darkness around his image.

He's asleep among the shadows is whispered over

and over and over again. It's a well wish they say to those mourning a loved one.

I hate it.

The enormous ballroom is overflowing with mourners. Fae I've never met before clasp my hand with tears in their eyes and remind me of what a "kind man" my brother was. *He's asleep among the shadows* they say so many times, it feels like an eerie threat.

"I think I'm going to be sick," I whisper when Zaviar brushes against my side.

It's the first thing I've said to him all day.

And it wipes away the pained look on his face. His hand pushes over his heart, and his tone is unsteady when he speaks. "You're strong. You can do this," he whispers.

My palm lifts to him to ask him if he's still hurting after my sister helped him, but he walks away once more.

"He's always walking away," I say beneath my breath.

"All the good ones do," Someone says behind me.

My dress skims the ground as I turn, and I'm surprised to meet the dark kind eyes of my father's advisor.

"Johnn," I say slowly.

All the good ones do.

What does that mean?

Just how many people hold demonic secrets in this castle? My father loved a demon. I recently found out my grandmother did, too.

What about you, Johnn? Are you in love with a monster my father has declared beneath us?

"The crowd has asked about King Gravier," Johnn says carefully.

198

I nod. He nods.

Neither of us say a treasonous word.

"Pen is going to greet them and give them an update on your father." His shoulders stiffen in his black suit, and if I wasn't certain of where he stands, I am now.

He's asked Pen to lie to these people.

Because he and I are on the same side.

"Good," I smile slowly, and I'm faintly aware of how close a demon is standing behind me.

"The man behind your throne, the one with the charred fingers and tattoos . . . he's looking at me like he wants to kill me." He takes a slow sip of his wine as tells me all of this in the most discreet way.

"Krave is a little . . . *protective.*" I smile as if it's nothing, but jealousy turns rather quickly for my incubus. One minute he's laughing and making sex jokes, the next he's eating all the happiness from the depths of your soul.

It happens.

I wave Johnn away with a smile before it can *happen* to my innocent advisor.

That false smile is still glued hard in place when my gaze spans to the small woman stepping up in front of the King's podium just ahead of us.

"Good Evening," Pen says solemnly. She's graceful, and her eyes shine with kindness. Everyone looks to her as a hush seizes the room. They trust her. "King Gravier," she clears her throat loudly before finding her tone, "King Gravier seems to have forgotten his son's memorial tonight. I've sent a messenger out to bring him home to his people, though. I'm sure he'll be with us shortly."

Sir Timmons' mouth falls open at that outright lie,

but I ignore him. Partly because Waltry doesn't appear very shocked. And partly because Johnn is staring hard at me. We all keep our composure and innocent appearances.

Murmurs fire through the watchful audience.

It's a scatter of nervous questions and speculations:

"He forgot?"

"He forgot his own son's memorial?"

"I heard he planned it. He requested this memorial. And now he's forgotten?"

"Well, I hear he's forgetting a lot of things these days."

"The apple doesn't fall far from Old Headless Hyval, eh?"

"Calm down," Pen says with a wave of her small hand.

"Calm down?" An elderly high fae asks with her blazing red wings fluttering. "Our King has forgotten us. Again. Forgotten his own children. This Kingdom needs guidance. Not a speaker!" The woman looks familiar, and it takes me a moment to remember her name from my childhood. She's Waltry's mate. I'm staring at her while her disgusted gaze holds on Pen for a long passing moment.

I let the time slip into the silence for several heartbeats before striding to Pen's side.

"Lady Charlotte, I can assure you, the Kingdom is not without guidance." I smooth the conversation and start to pull Pen away, taking a single step toward my mother, who sits without comment on all the chaos of her life.

"You have your mother's features," Lady Charlotte says, loud and clear. It brings a growing smile to my lips.

Because she's right on time.

"You have her strength, too. A true Princess of Roses," she calls out to me.

Yes. Yes, I am.

When the threads of my black gown sweep over the gleaming tile, the entire room is looking at me with big shining eyes. My chin tilts higher, my back straightening beneath their heavy attention.

This isn't a memorial.

It never was.

It's a revolution. The end of an era. And the beginning of a new fucking reign.

"Thank you," I say with a touch of humble kindness.

My lips part to say the speech I've prepared. The one that announces me as more than just a Princess. But a Queen this lost Kingdom needs.

Too bad those words never come out.

A door bangs open with slamming anger.

Big boots thunder over the tile, and I peer back and meet blazing silver eyes.

Eyes just like mine.

Fuck.

"You had a memorial for my only son. Without. Me." The King yells. The words boom over the fine wine glasses the guests hold and I note how many women just flinched from the sound of their King's voice.

He storms toward me in three big steps, and I'm going to fire whoever the hell was supposed to take him to his little doctor's checkup today.

"Father," I whisper, searching for words and lies lost in my head.

"Your Highness, you planned the memorial," Johnn

says slowly but loudly enough for all to hear.

My head turns. As does every-fucking-one else's.

"Wow," Damien whispers from behind me.

I fucking agree.

Wow.

"I—" Father stammers, and it's just enough time for Johnn to keep going.

"Everyone forgets sometimes, My King," the young advisor says with a sympathetic smile that says a thousand words.

It starts those murmurs right back up.

As for King Gravier, his face is so fucking red, I swear it's about to burst with how much raging blood is flowing through his veins.

He's going to kill Johnn.

But you have to be King to give that kind of order.

"Father. Why don't you give the announcement we've been discussing for our kingdom," I tell him with a peaceful tone, but gods, is he turning redder? Is that even possible?

"Aries," he warns on that growling tone, "I banished you once," he says lowly.

I swallow hard. A warm hand slides over mine, and I don't look back at the men I know are standing directly behind me.

"Darling, don't talk about that right now," a serene voice says.

Then her hand is on my shoulder. It's a touch filled with memories I can't explain. It's love, and it's comfort in one simple pat of the hand. That's just the magic a mother has, I guess.

I just didn't expect to ever feel it again.

"You promised Aries the crown, sweetheart," Mother says.

"I did no such thing!" His entire body shakes with outrage.

Zaviar takes one step, and he stands just in front of me but not blocking the sight of my father's blazing aggression from over the three thrones.

We're momentarily distracted when my mother pulls the shining sword hanging just behind my father's throne.

The crowning sword.

"I know. I know it's hard to remember everything." Even I'm stunned by my mother's words. "Just—give her the crown, Gravier. You and I can live along the river. We can rest and relax. We can let the days pass us by." She extends her small hands to offer my father the sword.

The anger on his face has turned to seething rage. A vein pulses at the center of his forehead.

He has to know this is the best option. The Shadow Guard will kill him. He'll die by their hand. Or he can go fuck off and die in silence, with the peaceful waters of the Iris River lulling him to sleep each night.

Sometimes, when we do the best thing for someone, it's still cruel. I don't think he's realized that until right now.

I take a slow stalking step closer. Zaviar's hand slides down mine, but I walk on until I'm right in front of my father. His long silver hair touches mine as I glare up into his eyes, but I keep my obedient daughter smile pressed firmly in place as I whisper to him and him alone, "How does it feel to finally be on the banishing end of banishment, Daddy?"

And then he does snap.

His composure breaks right down the middle, like ancient glass in a hail storm.

Magic flies out of him in splinters of deep gray that slap into me and send me backward, falling from the platform and skittering over the ballroom floor.

My back hits hard, and my breath leaves fast. I stare up at the high arching ceiling, taking a moment for the gasps of the people surrounding me to fully take effect. It's nothing but the sound of stunned shock.

It's a nice charming little sound in this moment of uprising.

I spot my mother also fallen to the floor. The crowning sword lies at her side, and there's a small scratch on her cheek, but she's unharmed for the most part.

When I stand, I don't expect to see what my wide eyes are taking in.

But there it is:

Krave's glittering black fingers arch sharply as he throws the King's enormous body against the wall just near the door without ever touching him. He pins the man there with nothing but dark demon magic.

The kind I've never seen.

"What is he?" A woman hisses at my side.

I have no fucking idea.

"Forgive me, My Former King, but," Krave bows formally as he keeps his mystical power held in place, "if you ever touch our Queen like that again, I will rip each of your limbs off one by one, Your Highness."

Zaviar's arms are folded hard across his chest, and his brother's stance mirrors his exactly. Even Ryke looks like he's about to climb the wall just to murder the King.

Things . . . have gotten a bit off-track here.

"Everything's fine," I say calmly.

I have *got* to keep hold of the calm. It has to stay in place. For everyone's sake.

"She's not your Queen!" Father roars, lashing against the magic that binds him.

Krave's hand twists just slightly, and sparkling black smoke wafts out, pressing toward the man held high above us. "Crown her," Krave commands.

A choking cough shakes from my father's broad chest, but he shakes his head hard as he gasps for a breath. The crowd shifts on their feet, and I can't stand here quietly any longer.

"Krave, put him down," I yell as several guards in shining uniforms start to close in on the demon.

"Call her your Queen," Krave says so loudly, it drowns out my voice.

Another stern shake of the King's head has a small wave of pent-up magic crashing out of the powerful incubus. It climbs high into the air, it picks up strength, it whirls violently with a sound of magic I've never heard before. It reaches the ceiling, causing the crowd to stumble back from the height of the ominous wave. It grows and grows and grows.

Before foreign slicing black light shoots through the room. It streams in on jagged blades and lands with a sinking thump.

Right into my father's chest.

Screams and running footsteps sound through the room as deep crimson blood pools at the center of the King's abdomen. Krave drops my father immediately. He hits with a resounding thump.

But Krave didn't do this. Crashing panic fills the room as my gaze scans the area for the attacker.

Long black fuming hair and a sinister smile step into view.

"It's midnight, sister," Corva says with too much calm and too much happiness.

"*No.*" It's the only word I can find in my mind, and it repeats over and over and over again.

The room clears in seconds, but all of the advisors, all of the guards, Sev, Isabella, and several onlookers watch hesitantly as the dark demon fae climbs the platform stairs toward my father's throne.

"In the event of the King's death, the eldest heir shall rule," Corva says, skimming her palms down her dress, looking down at her small crowd, and then taking her seat in my father's chair.

Mother is still staring vacantly at the blood pooling around her husband's body. No tears fall from her cheeks. No love is lost here.

But astonishment is fully in place.

"Ryke," my attention stays on the dangerous woman before me, "Take my mother and take Pen and get them out of here," I instruct with fraying calmness.

He pauses, his attention splicing from me to my sister and then back again. Then he does as I ask and guides the two women out the door and down the hall.

"You cannot rule," Johnn tells her, like a man who's far too advised for his own good.

"Johnn," he looks to me. "Shut up," I whisper, and his brows pull low over his brown eyes.

"You're a banished woman with no title. You cannot inherit your father's crown. Only a blood-born Sinclaire of royal title can be Queen. There are rules!" Johnn steps forward, and that's all it takes. That one little step.

And the room explodes with power. Black magic cuts out in inky colors. I shove the advisor out of the way, but the slicing energy hits Waltry straight through his eye. I don't have time to find the breath in my lungs as my wings splay out, and I catch the air. I'm soaring down on her in seconds. My hands hit her shoulders and the force of my attack sends the solid throne to its back. With deadly intent, she shoves me off her, but we both go scattering across the floor.

"You can't harm me," I scream at her.

"And neither can you," she hisses back, clawing at my hair for some sort of leverage as we grapple against one another. "But my friends can," she adds with a manic smile.

I blink at her for several seconds.

And then a buzzing sound stings through the air. A thousand sharp needles pierce my skin. A scream tears from my throat, and I slap at the tiny insects, but there are too many of them.

"Pixies," Damien whispers.

His big palms catches a few, and a cracking wet sound follows as he fists his hands together hard. Glitter slides through his knuckles. But there are so, so many more.

As I scream and kick and slap at the vile little creatures, a groan hums through a man just two feet from me.

Corva's knee comes up over and over again right between Zaviar's legs as he holds her by her throat against the ground. His arms tremble, but he never lets her go.

Until that lethal magic of hers slices out. It cuts through him, and I scream out with too much emotion in my voice as he falls to her side.

Krave, Damien, the King's guard, and the Shadow Guard rush the flurry of pixies and my powerful sister. Damien's big black wings fan out, and he tackles the demon fae to the ground with so much force, the floor shakes beneath me.

Smoke and magic burn through the room. It fills my lungs and attacks me just as much as the pixies slicing their swords into my flesh.

Blood coats my skin. I run as fast as I can, and when I find one more of the men I care about bleeding out from Corva's magic, the bond inside me rips open with newfound rage.

Just as Johnn said, there are rules.

And mate magic, it overrules vow magic.

I slink into the shadows along the wall. I black out the candles there, until a dense darkness covers me like a blanket. I use the unseen shadow magic for my own use. I use it to ink closer and closer and closer.

Before lurching forward. The sword in my hand is striking, it sweeps down with power and intent. The blade lands hard. It lodges deep. The inky smoke around me is too thick for me to see where I struck her at.

But I know I struck her.

The wafting black fog clears little by little. It funnels through the room and is collected from the source it originated from:

My sister. She stands in front of me with Damien

gasping at her feet, his face bloody but his body intact. The sword protrudes from her, sticking out at a sharp angle from her back. She smiles at me.

Confusion falls across my face, and when she turns, the tip of the blade is embedded into her back. But her black dress that covers her spine is a wavering color. It's . . . translucent.

Smoke.

"I'm made of smoke magic, sweet sister." She wretches the blade from her body, pulling the weapon straight through her stomach and out her front in an alarming way. "And *you*—you just broke our vow."

Her arm comes straight back, and she rails the sharp tip of the blade straight through my stomach in the blink of an eye.

The air in my lungs catches. Warmth seeps over my hands as they shakily slide down the front of my gown. The fabric becomes darker. And my palms become slicker.

The fighting rages on around me as I struggle to keep a breath in my lungs. Damien and Krave battle shimmering pixies. Light reflects in their eyes.

They'll never know how incredibly handsome they are when they're determined.

Ryke . . . he's safe. He's safe for now.

Zaviar . . .

I fall to my knees but try to search him out. What happened after he was struck down. Where is he? Is he alive?

"Hey, Pretty Crow." A deep voice is laced with pain as someone falls to their knees in front of me.

Zaviar's dark lashes flutter to keep his deep blue eyes

focused on me. His palm shakes against his chest, and blood coats the front of him, just like it does me.

We're both fucked.

We're both going to die, and no one can save us. We'll die with death all around us.

He'll leave his brother after all this time. And I'll leave my mates. I guess—I guess they won't be my mates after I'm gone.

I never even told Ryke.

I didn't get a chance to tell Damien I loved him. I love him so fucking much.

I never told Zaviar that I heard what he said that night.

There's so much I never told them.

But I have this moment. This one last moment.

"Zaviar," I whisper, and blood slides over my lips.

"Don't talk, Crow," he says as his cold hands slide around me. He holds me against his chest, and I stare out over his smooth shoulder. Pink feathers fan up in a way that block my view of the destruction.

"You never let me change your wings back," I say with weakness clinging to my tone.

A laugh shakes through him, and a hard cough follows the sweet sound of his amusement.

"That's your last fuckin' words, huh?"

A smile almost touches my lips.

"I don't want you to die with pink wings, Zaviar." My fingers skim over the soft downy feathers.

"Don't," he says, taking my hand and sliding his fingers slickly through mine.

I just look up at him as a breath rattles from my

lungs.

"It's the only thing that makes me feel like I'm yours," he hisses through his teeth as his body starts to shiver.

"*Mine*?" I almost choke on that word, but it fills me with warmth when there's so much coldness trying to sink in.

He nods his head slowly, tilting forward until our foreheads touch, and we breathe in each other's final breaths.

"*Mine*," I whisper once more with finality, my lashes closing with so much heaviness.

"*Yours*," he says like a sweet goodbye.

My body slackens as I slump into him. I feel his hold on me loosen as my heartbeat thumps once more in my ears.

. . .

Finally.

I find peace.

CHAPTER TWENTY-TWO
The Other Monsters
Zaviar

Warmth scalds across my skin. It burns like frostbite being dunked into hot water.

Long hair tangles in my hand, and I know who it is just from the way she hums softly against my neck.

I smile slowly and hold her harder against me. I've seen the realm of the gods, and yet, nothing's ever felt as good as her body does against mine.

"Who the fuck is that?" A familiar voice asks with disdain infecting her tone.

My eyes open slowly.

Piercing bright whiteness surrounds me, and my stomach sinks hard.

I pull Aries's naked body up closer against mine. Her stark black wings draw attention from the few people watching us as we sit amidst a soft white fog.

"I said, who the fuck did you bring here, Zaviar?" The shrill voice asks once more.

My throat tightens as I look up at the woman in a long white gown. Her golden wings shine in the intense lighting.

"Mira, how did I get here?" I ask the angriest valkyrie the gods have ever created.

Her golden eyes glare down on me with the heat of a thousand suns. I sit at her feet with nothing but big pink wings to cover my nudity. I use my wings instead to shield Aries from view of the others the best I can.

"You died, you dumb fuck." She shifts on her feet, her smooth arms folding hard over her chest. "And when you returned back to your realm, you brought trash in with you. Get up and get her registered before Darine spots you."

Fuccck.

The memory of white horns and crawling magic sends a spider-like shiver down my spine as I hold Aries harder against my chest. I hold her like I can protect her from cruel magic like she's never seen before.

I hope she never wakes. Not here.

Because she's about to find out that some monsters are blessed by the gods.

And I'm one of them.

The End

ALSO BY A.K. KOONCE
Reverse Harem Books

The Hopeless Series
Hopeless Magic
Hopeless Kingdom
Hopeless Realm
Hopeless Sacrifice

The To Tame a Shifter Series
Taming
Claiming
Maiming
Sustaining
Reigning

The Origins of the Six Series
Academy of Six
Control of Five
Destruction of Two

The Royal Harem Series
The Hundred Year Curse
The Curse of the Sea
The Legend of the Cursed Princess

The Harem of Misery Series
Pandora's Pain

The Severed Souls Series
Darkness Rising
Darkness Consuming
Darkness Colliding

The Huntress Series
An Assassin's Death
An Assassin's Deception
An Assassin's Destiny

The Villainous Wonderland Series
Into the Madness
Within the Wonder
Under the Lies

Paranormal Romance
The Cursed Kingdoms Series
The Cruel Fae King
The Mortals and Mystics Series
Fate of the Hybrid, Prequel
When Fate Aligns, Book one
When Fate Unravels, Book two
When Fate Prevails, Book three

Standalone Novels
Hate Me Like You Do
Resurrection Island

Printed in Great Britain
by Amazon